TO SEEK AND TO FIND

Enchanting Encounters, Book One

Tamryn Eradani

"Project Notice Me" is a win-win for Kyle. He'll do a series of demonstrations at the club and have a good time with people he knows and the fledging Doms who are new to the scene and looking for encouragement from an experienced Sub. And maybe along the way, he'll attract the attention of the new Dom at the club, the one with terrible taste in fashion, but who has the most intense focus Kyle has ever seen. He wants the entirety of the man's attention on him. The clothes are optional.

A NineStar Press Publication

Published by NineStar Press
P.O. Box 91792,
Albuquerque, New Mexico, 87199 USA.
www.ninestarpress.com

To Seek and to Find

ISBN: 978-1-947904-97-2

Printed in the USA
First Edition
January, 2018

Also available in eBook, ISBN: 978-1-947904-93-4

Warning: This book contains sexually explicit content, which may only be suitable for mature readers.

Chapter One

"SO," KYLE SAYS. He slinks into Jenny's office, glad he wore his stretchy jeans when he pulls a chair out from the table and turns it around so he can straddle it. Even with the give in his jeans, they still pull tight across his quads.

Jenny doesn't glance up from her computer.

"Remember that time I introduced you and Charlotte?" Kyle asks, undeterred by her obvious disinterest in him. He and Jenny have been best friends for what seems like forever, and they both work from their apartments—Jenny does photography, Kyle does graphic design—and if she didn't want to be bothered, then she would've closed her office door.

As it is, she'd left it wide open, and Kyle is happy to take advantage.

At the mention of Charlotte's name, Jenny looks up, a smile on her face. They've been together for five years, but her expression always softens whenever Charlotte's mentioned as though they've only been dating for a few weeks. Kyle thinks it's sickeningly cute. He hopes one day someone will look like that when *his* name is brought up.

Jenny registers the rest of what Kyle's said, and her smile is replaced with something more guarded, suspicious. "Last time you opened with that, we almost wound up in jail."

"Exaggeration," Kyle says.

"The time before that you made me go bungee jumping with you."

"That was awesome." There's nothing like the rush of adrenaline as he plummeted toward the earth. Then, right when he thought his harness was going to fail and he would splat, it caught him with a jerk of reassurance. Kyle had loved it. Jenny...not so much.

"I'm afraid of heights."

"Which meant you were incredibly brave on top of being a good friend." Kyle needs to get to the point. He's on a break from his work because all shades of red now look the same to him, but he has a project to finish before the day is over. "This is a favor that'll benefit us both."

Jenny continues to look skeptical.

"I want you to tie me up," he says.

Kyle and Jenny have been roommates, have worked together, and have scened together throughout their long and storied friendship. They've never slept together because Kyle's bisexual, and while Jenny enjoys men on an aesthetic basis, she prefers sex with women.

They frequent the same club, Enchanting Encounters. Jenny does rope demos and occasionally ties up a close friend, but she isn't as involved with the casual scene as Kyle. She's been pulling away since she met Charlotte, going mostly to keep Kyle company or catch up with their friends there.

Kyle, on the other hand, is still searching for someone who wants him for more than a couple of sessions a month. He wants a Dom who wants him back, and so far, he hasn't had any luck. He's hoping his luck is about to change.

Jenny abandons even the pretense of working. "Is this about the new guy?"

He grins. "Who else?"

Kyle spends a lot of time at Enchanting Encounters. Working from home means he's able to set his own schedule, which allows him to sleep in after a night of play or take an early afternoon if that's what works better with his partner's schedule.

Sometimes, he'll go to the club to have a drink or chat with his friends, but more often he's there with the intent to pick-up or because he's part of a demo.

Last week, things got interesting because there was a new guy.

The BDSM world is a small one, and Kyle has known most of the people at Enchanting Encounters for years now. Someone will bring a friend sometimes or someone will move into the area or move away, but it doesn't happen often, which means it's always exciting when there's a new face.

Unfortunately, it also means there's a lot of competition for the man's attention, and Kyle needs a battle plan.

The first time Kyle saw New Guy, it was a normal Friday night and he had a drink in hand as he did a sweep of the bar to see if anyone caught his eye. He hadn't come in with a particular scene in mind. Some nights, that made it easier to find a partner while other nights it made it more difficult.

That Friday had been a difficult night. Since he wasn't sure what he wanted, no one popped out at him. If he wanted a good spanking, then Renee was his go-to, but he wasn't feeling it. Same with a bit of bondage and a pegging, which is what Alexa would give him. Dylan was strutting around in his full leather gear, but Kyle wasn't in the mood to have to work, and Dylan always makes him work.

The only person who drew his interest was TJ, Kyle's favorite bartender, and while TJ flirts with anyone who seems receptive, he doesn't have sex with club members. It's a shame, but Kyle can respect his choice.

Kyle was considering a second drink when his eyes landed on someone at the far end of the bar. New Guy was, well, new, which immediately made him interesting. What kept his attention was the expression on the guy's face as he talked with Lou.

The guy was completely captivated even though Kyle knows from personal experience that Lou isn't the most interesting person to talk to. Lou's gorgeous, especially when he has red welts against his almost inhumanly pale skin, but he's not the most thrilling conversationalist.

Still, New Guy leaned in like nothing in the world could pull him away.

Part of the reason Kyle scenes is he loves having the full attention of another person on him. If New Guy can be that intense during a conversation, then Kyle wants to find out what he's like in a scene.

He didn't look away from Lou once, didn't give Kyle a chance to catch his eye, and Kyle eventually had to move on. He didn't go home with anyone Friday night. A couple of people approached him, but he turned them down. New Guy was the only person on his mind, and it wouldn't be fair to anyone he scened with.

Anyway, Kyle didn't have a chance to talk to New Guy on Friday night, but he's determined to change that. The guy is attractive and he has the kind of focus Kyle craves.

"You're not the only one asking about him," Jenny says.

Kyle shrugs. "He'll want me once he sees me."

"Modest. So, what's your big plan, do a bunch of demos until he wanders over to see one?"

That's exactly his plan.

Jenny groans. "Are you serious?"

"It's a good plan! I'm hot, I'm an incredible sub. And while I'm waiting for him to notice me, I'll be doing scenes I like. Plus, Wanda's been after me to do some more demos. I'm good for business." Kyle doesn't bother holding back his smirk.

Jenny reaches across her table to shove his face away. "You're terrible."

"But you're going to help me."

Jenny sighs. "Because you got me and Charlotte together? That won't work as leverage forever."

"You're going to help me because you just got a new order of rope in, and you know I look gorgeous in lavender."

"Ugh. Fine. I'll do a demo with you. But you'll let me tie you up for a photoshoot. *Unpaid.*"

Kyle doesn't bother to hold back his grin as he says, "Deal."

"I'll hang you upside down," Jenny threatens.

It's an idle threat. She likes to suspend him, but usually not upside down.

"You're the best," Kyle tells her. He stands up, smacks a kiss to her cheek, and leaves to finish the rest of his project. He needs to be on top of his work this week, or he won't have the time to hang around the club and put Project: Notice Me into effect.

IT TAKES TWO weeks for Kyle and Jenny to get around to their scene. It feels like an interminable wait to Kyle, but they're both busy, and Jenny is a meticulous planner. She's tying him up because they're friends, but she'll do it well because she takes pride in her work.

Kyle can't fault her for a good work ethic even if patience isn't one of his better qualities.

"I saw people are using bamboo poles in their bondage," Jenny says when Kyle meets her at Enchanting Encounters.

Jenny's in black leggings and an oversized white T-shirt which slips off one shoulder to show off her pink bra strap and the outward edges of one of her tattoos. When she does demos like this, she keeps her outfits plain so the focus is on her model and the art she creates rather than herself. If she was here to be social, then she'd be wearing something more colorful and daring.

"You're trying something new with an audience?"

It's a surprise because Jenny doesn't like to be anything but her best in front of a crowd and doing something new always runs the risk of doing something wrong. Or, more likely in her case, doing something that isn't perfectly pleasing to the eye.

Jenny is all about aesthetics.

"Of course not," Jenny says. "I might try it for our private shoot, though."

"Sure."

She raises her eyebrows at his easy acquiescence and pushes further. "Will you dye your hair?"

Kyle laughs.

He's never dyed his hair in his life, not when all his friends bleached theirs in high school and not when some of his fellow subs were experimenting with cotton candy pinks and cherry slushie reds to try to draw attention to them.

He's kept his natural black hair his entire life, and as much as he loves Jenny, he won't alter it for her.

"Maybe a wig then," Jenny says.

Kyle pouts as he slings an arm around her shoulders, only a bit of a reach since she forewent her heels tonight. "Aren't I beautiful just the way I am?"

She smacks his ass. "Get ready and meet me in the show room when you're done."

The show room is exactly that, a big room which can be converted to show off different aspects of BDSM. It's large enough to hold several demos at a time, but tonight Kyle and Jenny are the only show on the schedule.

The room is as familiar to him as the play rooms, though those are generally reserved for the scene partners or, in some cases, small invited parties. In the show room, anyone is invited to wander down from the bar and watch.

It's like a karaoke night except with less public humiliation. Well, depending on the scene.

Kyle showered before heading over to the club, which means all he needs to do now is strip out of his jeans and T-shirt and put them in his locker. He puts his shoes on top of his folded clothes and stuffs his socks inside his shoes so he won't lose them.

The only thing he leaves on is his briefs, plain and black so they won't distract from Jenny's rope work.

He checks himself in front of the mirror to make sure he looks presentable. He skims a hand down his chest and frowns as he pats his abs. He needs to make sure he goes to the gym three, if not four, times a week if he wants to keep his definition up. There are people out there to impress, and he needs to look his best.

Next, he runs his hands through his hair to mess it up. It's long enough for someone to grip it if they work hard enough, but it isn't floppy and it doesn't fall into his eyes. He only tried that look briefly because it was a pain in the ass to have to constantly flip his hair out of his eyes.

Right now, his eyes are bright, excited for what's about to happen, and his cheeks are already flushed.

Tonight will be a good night.

By the time he wanders into the show room, a crowd has gathered. Jenny and Kyle teaming up is enough to draw a good number of people, and for those who didn't know this was happening tonight, word must have spread fast downstairs because he sees plenty of people with partially drunk drinks in hand as if they'd been pulled away from whatever's going on upstairs.

Kyle grins at Renee, waves to Alexa, and winks at a cute guy he's seen around, but hasn't gotten to know yet. The guy blushes, but he doesn't break eye contact, and his chest puffs up like he's pleased Kyle's noticed him.

Kyle allows his gaze to linger because if one little wink is enough to pull this kind of reaction, then he wants to see what he can do with a bit more effort.

"Quit flirting," Jenny says, voice low enough just for Kyle's ears. "You're mine now."

All the air whooshes out of Kyle's body, and he has to lean into Jenny so she'll steady him. It catches him off-guard every time his best friend makes the switch from easygoing friend to commanding Domme.

His body's still loose, still relaxed, but he ducks his head in deference, his way of signaling he's ready, and that she has all his focus until she ends the scene.

"Good," she says, and the word stirs something warm in him. "Lie down."

She motions to the padded platform that's been set up at the bottom of the small well. Kyle walks down three stairs to reach it, the purpose being that people can gather around the edges of the stairs and look down to see everything Jenny's doing without being in Jenny's way or each other's.

"On your back," Jenny says.

Kyle lies down and blinks against the sharpness of the overhead lights.

"Can someone dim those?" Jenny asks, pointing to the lights. "Or turn them so they're not right in his face?"

A moment later, the light fixtures tilt so Kyle can look up without being blinded. Jenny joins him in the well, and the platform puts him at waist level for her so she can work with ease.

She runs a hand through his hair, smiling as he pushes into the touch.

"You good?" she asks.

"Yeah."

With someone else, he'd add a cheeky comment but not with Jenny. Jenny doesn't like to work to bring a sub down. She'll work *for* her sub, and Kyle will fight anyone who says otherwise, but she doesn't want to struggle with them. She wants them to go down because they trust her.

Kyle enjoys a bit of a struggle. He likes to see where the limits are and what his Dom will do to enforce them and how much leeway he has. He likes to push so he can feel someone push back, but that's for personal play.

When he's with Jenny, Kyle's on his very best behavior because they're friends and she deserves him at his best. Especially on a night like tonight when she's doing him a favor. He won't be difficult for her.

There's still the itch under his skin that makes him want to twitch or squirm, to move out of the position she arranges him in so she'll use a firmer hand. She guides him where she wants him to be. Her touch is too light for what he likes and doesn't linger long enough, but he reminds himself he'll have rope soon.

Rope to hold him still, to hold him down, to keep him where he needs to be.

It isn't his favorite, but he can work with it.

Jenny flicks his forehead. "Am I boring you?" she asks, eyes slightly narrowed.

Realizing his thoughts have wandered, Kyle shakes his head and says, "Sorry."

He refocuses as Jenny bends down to retrieve her spool of rope. It's lavender, as promised, and he hears a few murmurs of approval in the crowd. Kyle allows the sound to drift through him and it warms him, settles him.

It's no secret he enjoys an audience and scening with Jenny means she'll transform him into a masterpiece, framed for everyone to stare at and admire.

Heat flashes through him, and it makes him gasp before the feeling settles low in his belly. He *wants*. When he and Jenny scene in private, he rarely grows hard, but it's different when they're in public. He wants to reach down and adjust himself, but he knows better than to disturb the picture Jenny's creating.

"That's better," Jenny murmurs. She runs her hand through his hair again and tilts his head back so she can look at him.

He opens himself up to her gaze so she can see every thought passing through his head. He wants her to know he's enjoying this because it means she's doing a good job. It's a subtle check-in, but it's one they both need so she can begin.

When Jenny lifts the end of her rope, the room seems to draw a collective breath, waiting to see what she'll do with it.

She begins with Kyle's waist. Kyle can't see what she's doing—he keeps her eyes on her face not her hands—but he can feel it. She loops the rope around once then does it again. Her fingers brush against his skin. She does something different, but a brief look from Jenny makes him stop trying to puzzle it out.

It's not his job to anticipate her design. It's not his job to see it. His job is to *be* it. He trembles, a small movement no one will see. It's one Jenny can feel, though, and she pauses long enough to drag her knuckles against the taut skin of his stomach.

"You're good," she promises. "I've got you."

He dips his head in a barely perceptible nod, and she continues to wind her rope. She secures him with her rope and her touch and her words. He finds comfort in allowing her to work her design, in handing full trust over to her.

He doesn't know how long she works on the waist piece, but he knows when she finishes it because the rope winds higher. The waist piece feels like a corset, maybe not as tight, but still tight enough to know it's there. It's Jenny's way of saying *I was here. I'm still here,* even as she moves to the next section.

It's a struggle to keep his eyes open when all he wants to do is sink into the spell she's weaving, but he promised her his complete focus.

She leans over him as she loops the rope around the back of his neck twice, like a halter. It brings her closer and, more importantly, makes her the only thing he can see. There are no distractions, just the glint as the light catches her piercings and her hands, deft as they work.

When she moves to his arms, she slows down, her touch more careful because she knows he isn't the biggest fan of restraints unless he's being restrained by a person.

It's been several years now, but early in his kink days, he had a partner secure him to the headboard and leave the room. Kyle hadn't been able to follow him, hadn't been able to free himself, and the panic rose sharp and quick, and he's never been able to shake the experience.

There's no panic now. Jenny won't leave him alone. Even when she's finished tying him up, she'll stay at his side.

Her next design brings her close to him again, and he turns his head to press a kiss to the back of her hand. She pauses, a smile of her own flickering across her features before she returns to work.

She finishes her design and steps back to look, but she keeps one hand on his shoulder, a point of contact for him to hold onto, a reminder that she isn't leaving. Kyle drags his gaze up to meet hers and watches as she glances over what she's done.

She nods to herself, pleased, and it makes Kyle puff up, proud, even though he didn't do anything but lie here.

"Beautiful," Jenny says, and he doesn't know if she's referring to him or her design or both. "Are you ready for people to come down?"

Kyle nods. This is his favorite part, when the audience is allowed down to see Jenny's work up close. Some people only want to look, others want to ask Jenny questions, and some want to be closer to Kyle.

"Vets know the drill," Jenny says, pitching her voice louder. Her hand stays on Kyle's shoulder. "You can come down and look. You can even touch, but Kyle won't talk to you or look at you. Any questions you have, you can ask me. Don't be shy but don't overstep."

There's a bit of a threat there at the end, and Kyle smiles at her standing guard over him. His protector.

He doesn't look away from Jenny, even as he hears footsteps and the soft mutterings of the crowd. Jenny's the one who did this to him, who drew everyone's interest. Most of these people may be here for Kyle, but Kyle's here for Jenny.

He shrugs his shoulder as best he can with his bindings, pushing into Jenny's touch. She glances down at him, and he smiles. There's nothing's wrong; he just wants her to know he appreciates her. She shakes her head, but she also runs a hand through his hair so she can't be too upset.

The first outside touch comes as a surprise because Kyle had forgotten for a moment there were people besides him and Jenny in the room. Two fingers tap against his ankle, nowhere near any of the rope. It startles him, his body remaining still, his brain twitching instead.

The haze in his mind clears for a moment, the lights around him suddenly sharper as the world threatens to come back in full force. He doesn't want it yet, but he doesn't know how to make it stop.

Jenny runs her hand through his hair again, guiding him back down. She knows what he wants and knows how to make sure he has it. If she was anyone else, then he'd turn his head and try to press a kiss against her wrist in a thank-you. Maybe he'd even beg for a stronger hold in his hair.

But this is Jenny, his best friend, and they aren't like that.

The hand on his ankle trails up to his knee.

Kyle's legs aren't bound, only his top half is, which means he could spread his legs if he wanted, and encourage the hand to reach higher.

"He's good, isn't he?" Jenny asks. "He doesn't even need the rope to keep him still. He just looks too pretty in it for me not to tie him up."

I'm good. Kyle's restlessness settles into something more languid. *I'm good and good means keeping still.*

The hand climbs higher, anyway, until fingers play at the edge of his briefs. Everyone here knows better than to go farther. One of the rules, when he plays with Jenny, is that he can't come during the scene—by her hands or anyone else's.

Another set of hands find him, and Kyle tips his head back as a finger dips beneath the rope around his waist to test how tight it is. Or maybe they want to feel the indents of the rope on his skin. Jenny doesn't tie him tight—this is decorative rather than restrictive—but there's always a light impression of the rope when she unwinds him.

The marks never last long, and in the moment, it disappoints him. Once he's come back to himself, he doesn't mind as much. As much as he loves Jenny, it isn't her marks he wants to carry on him, soft impressions made by softer rope.

He longs for bruises that say *I was here* and maybe, one day, a collar which says *He is mine.*

But those are thoughts for another time because Jenny can't give him any of those things, and even if she could, he doesn't want them from her.

More hands are on him now. Chilled fingers touch his shoulders, a callused finger taps his lip, the heel of someone's hand drags against the strip of skin between the rope and his briefs.

No one but Jenny touches his hair.

There are voices, too. *Pretty. Gorgeous.* When Kyle's face flushes he hears *Responsive* and *He's so good for you.* He wants to close his eyes and sink into the praise. Instead, he wraps the words around him, allowing them to warm him from the inside out as he gazes up at Jenny.

She's the one who made him pretty, the one who put him on display for everyone to see.

Everyone?

He wants to look around and see if New Guy is in the crowd. Is the strong hand on his thigh New Guy? Is the soft voice that praises Kyle's coloring him? Is he hanging back and just watching, too shy to approach Kyle?

Does he see Kyle as he is—an offering?

Kyle draws in a sharp breath before he plummets—down, down, down. The hands on him burn through his skin, but it isn't enough. He wants them to press harder, to dig until he can really feel it. He wants to beg them to touch him until it's too much and he begs them to stop.

He wants—

"Hey there," Jenny says. Her hand is firm in his hair and she gives his head a shake as if he's an errant puppy.

Kyle opens his eyes to see her leaning over him. When did his eyes close? Jenny doesn't like him to close his eyes. He didn't listen. He isn't good. He—

"Hey," Jenny says, insistent this time. "I've got you. You went pretty deep there, huh?"

Kyle blinks a few times, his eyelids heavy and dragging down. He glances around and sees everyone's cleared out so it's only him and Jenny here.

"Fuck," he says, and his voice sounds like someone rubbed his throat with sandpaper.

"Hell of a compliment." She smiles as if she can soften the roiling emotions inside him. "Are you good for me to untie you?"

"Yeah."

He's glad he doesn't have to do anything but stay still as she undoes her work. Normally, this is one of his favorite parts of the night, watching as each coil comes undone, as Jenny undoes each knot with practiced hands.

On most nights, it feels like he's emerging from a cocoon.

Tonight, though, he feels as if she's untethering him. Will he float away as soon as the rope is gone?

This has never happened to him with Jenny before.

This is what happens when you think about other people while in a scene.

Guilt threatens to sour his mood, but Jenny's hands stay gentle as she finishes unwinding the rope and if she isn't angry with him then he shouldn't be angry with himself. Or should he?

Jenny helps him sit up, and she stands between his legs as she pulls a plain white T-shirt over his head. It's from a ten-pack bought at the store, and once he finds the arm holes, Jenny helps him with his jeans. Both the shirt and the jeans have seen enough washes to make them soft. It's a comfortable outfit, but it certainly isn't something he'd wear when he's trying to pick up.

Lastly, Jenny fastens a yellow bracelet around his wrist. He stares dumbly at it even though this is a standard part of his post-demo routine. The yellow tells the bartender he's not allowed anything with alcohol and it tells the other people at the club that he's off-limits for the rest of the night.

Usually, Kyle doesn't mind. He'll float during a demo, float after it, and soak up praise and appreciation while he nurses a cranberry juice. Then he'll go home and jerk off to the memories of the night.

He already knows that won't cut it tonight.

Cut it.

He glances down at his bracelet. When he was a dumbass teenager, he'd try to scrub the X off the back of his hand which warned people off buying him drinks. He knows better than to slip off the bracelet, though. Wanda would be pissed at him, maybe even ban him for a week, and he'd deserve it.

He scratches at the skin under the bracelet and glares at the bright yellow. The bracelet is a beacon to everyone in the club so they can conspire against him and make sure he doesn't get what he wants.

What he *needs*.

"Come on," Jenny says as she tugs Kyle off the bench. "Let's get you a drink."

It's part of his routine.

Routine is good, he reminds himself. *I know exactly what I can have tonight, and it will have to be enough.*

"You gonna buy it for me?" Kyle asks. He clings to Jenny's hand more than he holds it as she leads him to the bar. He flutters his eyelashes at her, over the top, and is rewarded when she laughs.

"Your charms don't work on me." She dumps him onto a seat and flags TJ over. "Can you get him a cranberry juice?"

Kyle turns his attention to TJ and gives him an all-too-obvious once-over. His curls look especially good tonight. "TJ can get me anything he wants."

TJ laughs as Jenny gives him her order, and Kyle knows TJ doesn't mean anything by it, but it feels like he's laughing *at* Kyle. Because Jenny and TJ are both immune to his charms, and even if TJ wasn't, Kyle can't go home with him. He can't go home with anyone, but he knows this is the kind of night where going home on his own won't be enough.

Kyle leans against Jenny's side as TJ returns with a cranberry juice for him and a beer for Jenny. He takes a sip of his juice—tart with a bit of a bite to it, which is why it's his post-scene drink of choice. It doesn't do anything for him tonight.

He needs more than juice and some friendly cuddling.

"We're going to talk about this," Jenny tells him. "Not tonight but soon. Just so you know."

Kyle nods. He knows they need to talk about it, even if he doesn't particularly want to. It's embarrassing to admit he wasn't at his best, and he doesn't want to talk through why, but he knows they will so they can try to make sure it doesn't happen again.

Renee wanders over to them, and Kyle gives her a once-over the same as TJ. She's in gunmetal gray skinny jeans tucked into knee-high boots with a wicked heel on them, and that's where his gaze is drawn. She's let him fuck her while she's wearing these boots, so he knows how good it feels to have the point of the heel dig into his back.

"Whoa, there," Renee says, laughing as she sits down next to him.

He doesn't want her laughing. He wants her to know he's serious. He lifts his gaze to meet hers so she can see everything he's thinking. He lets her see how much he wants her, how badly he needs a strong hand on him tonight.

He sways toward her, and the smile slips off her face. Her short fingernails tap against his cheek.

"That's how it is?" she asks.

Kyle turns to press a kiss against her fingertips.

"Hey," Jenny interjects. She tugs pointedly on Kyle's yellow bracelet.

Renee raises her eyebrows. "You're taking him home?" She tilts Kyle's face toward Jenny. "Look at him, he's not going home on his own tonight."

"He's with me," Jenny says, and she's turned to Renee now, challenging.

Caught between both women, Kyle frowns. This isn't how he likes being talked about. He doesn't mind people talking over him or talking to each other about him if it's nice things. He doesn't like being talked about as though he can't make his own decisions.

Kyle touches his fingers to Jenny's wrist to soften his next words. "I'm not going home with you. We don't do this, remember?"

"We *can*," Jenny says, stubborn. It comes from a good place, she wants to take care of him, but there's no point in them doing something neither of them will enjoy.

"You won't like it," Kyle says. He glances at Renee. "She will."

Jenny hesitates, her need to be responsible struggling with her need to give him what he wants. If it was anyone else, Kyle wouldn't push, but he's known Renee since he first started coming to Enchanting Encounters. She's the first Domme he ever had, and he trusts her. Jenny can too.

"Charlotte's waiting for you," Kyle says because their nights have a pattern. After their scene is over, Kyle goes home to jerk off and Jenny goes home to Charlotte. Everyone gets what they want. Kyle's the one who deviated from the script, and Jenny shouldn't suffer because of it.

"She'll understand."

"Please," Kyle says. "This is what I want."

Jenny's eyes dip back to his bracelet.

"I'll take care of him," Renee promises. "We can set up check-ins if it makes you more comfortable."

"Go to your place," Jenny tells Kyle. "That way if you need anything, I'll be right down the hall."

"Of course," Renee says. "Do you want to know the game plan?"

Jenny scrunches up her nose, and Kyle laughs.

Jenny points to Kyle. "You're making me lunch tomorrow."

"Yes."

Jenny looks between the two of them before she takes a deep breath. "All right. If you're both sure, but I want check-ins."

"You'll get them," Renee promises.

Jenny hesitates for one last moment before she pats Kyle's shoulder then leaves them be. As soon as she's gone, Kyle leans against Renee's side. She curls a hand around his neck; a steady touch, a promise that she's here now and will take care of him.

"Can we leave?" Kyle asks. Now that he knows there's a plan, anticipation bubbles up.

"Finish your juice."

There's enough command in her tone to make Kyle sit up straight. He swallows half his juice in one go, then Renee covers his glass with her free hand so he can't chug the rest.

"You went down hard," Renee says, and she sounds curious. "You don't usually do that with Jenny."

"Have never done it with Jenny," Kyle corrects her. He wishes he could take another sip of his drink because at least then he wouldn't be able to talk. But since he can't, he ends up asking, "Are you okay with sloppy seconds?"

Renee's nails dig into his neck, and there's nothing good about this pain. "Don't talk about yourself like that. You're not sloppy."

Kyle presses sticky lips to Renee's knuckles, seeking forgiveness, and her hand relaxes its hold. "Not sloppy *yet*," he says, a hint of hopefulness in his voice.

"Maybe." Renee's lips curl up in a smile. "Once you finish your juice, I'll drive us to your apartment, and once we're there, we can discuss what'll happen tonight. I want you more clearheaded."

Kyle's negotiated with Renee so many times they forgo it more often than not these days. There aren't many people he'll improv with, but he doesn't know many people the way he knows Renee. Tonight, he understands the need to talk it through. She didn't bring him down, so she doesn't know where his head is at.

"Yes, ma'am," Kyle says.

Renee squeezes the back of his neck again as she leans in. "You'll say that again tonight, but you'll mean it. Now, ask me if you can finish your juice."

Oh, fuck. Tonight's going to be a very good night.

Chapter Two

IT'S WEIRD TO bring someone back to his apartment for a scene. Kyle's deal with Wanda, where he does demos when she wants them and mentors new subs and works with new Doms, means he doesn't have to pay for his rooms at the club. He almost exclusively scenes at Enchanting Encounters because they have a wide variety of sets and toys and it makes check-ins easy. Plus, it's a good reminder of what kind of relationship he's in.

Leading a Dom into his apartment is something he wants, but Renee isn't right for him now. She's good to him, but she isn't The One. Jenny laughs at Kyle and his vague romantic notions, but she isn't searching anymore. She's already met the person who'll make her happy for the rest of her life.

Kyle's met plenty of people he wants to make happy, but he's met very few who don't end up taking advantage of that toward the end.

"I've lost you," Renee says.

Her voice snaps him back to the immediate present even though there's nothing sharp in it. Her tone is soft like she's *handling* him.

"Sorry," Kyle says. He waits for Renee to come in before he closes the door and turns the lock.

"You still good?" Renee catches his chin in her hand and tilts it down so she can look him in the eye.

"Still good. Still want you."

"Flatterer." She squeezes his chin before she drops her hand. "What happened tonight?"

"Standard rope demo, and then I slipped too deep." He glances up at Renee expecting censure, but she waves at him to continue. "Normally, I go home by myself and take care of things, but I know I need more than that tonight."

"What are you looking for?"

"I have a brush." He has a large collection of toys, actually. It's arranged on what he thinks is supposed to be a shoe shelf in his closet, but he has more sex toys than shoes. "I want you to hit me with it and then I want you to turn it around and use the bristles on me."

The bristles are stiff enough to scratch but not so stiff they'll draw blood. He shifts from foot to foot, already thinking about how it'll feel when she drags the bristles against his heated, sensitive skin.

He's not as floaty as he was at the club, but he wants Renee to take his world and narrow it down to small moments, to individual sensations. He wants to turn everything over to her and just follow where she leads him. He wants to be taken care of.

"After that?" Renee asks.

She's careful to keep her distance, careful she doesn't touch him now. Kyle knows it's because she doesn't want to influence his thoughts, but he still wants to be in contact. But if she had a hand on his cheek then he could read her reactions and know if she liked what he was talking about or if he needed to change direction.

Normally, Kyle doesn't have a problem laying out exactly what he wants, but what he wants more than anything right now is to please. He doesn't think Renee will ask anything of him he isn't willing to give her, but it's safest for them to stay apart until they've agreed on the plan for tonight.

"Something," Kyle answers. He hasn't thought this far. "I want to be on my back."

"You want to feel it even after I'm done spanking you?"

Kyle nods.

"Would you like me to fuck you after? Roll a condom on you and ride you?"

Kyle's eyes flutter shut as he imagines it—his ass burning from its recent abuse as she sinks down on him and *uses* him. Pain on one side of his body, pleasure on the other, twisting him up until he doesn't know what he wants.

"Yeah," Kyle answers, voice hoarse. "That sounds good."

Renee finally touches him, carding a hand through his hair, her nails scratching at his scalp. He moans and tilts his hand further into the touch. His legs tremble, but he wouldn't mind dropping to his knees for her in his living room. Maybe he could eat her out while he's down there. He'd make it good for her.

"I'm going to tell Jenny we're here," Renee says. "I want you naked and bent over your bed by the time I join you. Can you do that for me?"

"Yeah," he says.

The hand slips from his hair, and she slaps him lightly on the ass. "Go."

He goes.

He pulls his shirt off as soon as he's in his bedroom and tosses it into the overflowing laundry basket. He should take care of that tomorrow. Probably do his sheets too for good measure. He tugs his jeans off and folds them before putting them in their drawer. Next off are his briefs and his socks.

Naked now, he glances at his bed then into the hallway. He can't hear Renee, so he takes the extra minute to fetch his brush from his closet. He places it on his bed and arranges himself the way Renee asked.

He braces his arms on his bed and his feet on the floor, and it means he can't see his bedroom door. He'd have to turn and look over his shoulder, and Renee didn't tell him he could so he hangs his head between his arms and keeps his ears trained for the sound of Renee coming down the hall.

It doesn't take long for him to hear the click of her heels on the hardwood, and he can't help his shiver of anticipation. Once she's here, she'll take care of him, give him exactly what he needs.

He hears when she stops in the doorway and he arches his back, *presents* himself for her, and he can hear her low chuckle.

"Pretty as a picture," she tells him, voice growing louder as she approaches him. "Better than a picture, though. Pictures don't make sounds."

She runs her hands over his ass, nails dragging lightly over his skin before her thumbs smooth away the faint red lines she leaves behind. "Will you make sounds for me?"

"Yes."

"Good." She picks the brush up off the bed. "This is nice. I don't think I've seen it before. Is it new?"

"Had it for a while."

"A favorite, then? Something you keep hidden away?"

"Yeah. Guess that means you're pretty special."

"I already knew that, but thanks for the ego boost." She taps the back of the brush against the curve of his ass. "Are you ready?"

"Yeah."

Kyle spreads his legs another inch apart and leans forward so he can rest his forehead on his bed. It's the best way to make sure he doesn't wake up tomorrow with a sore neck. A sore ass is expected, he's even looking forward to it, but he wants the rest of him to feel good.

The first hit of the brush catches him off-guard. It doesn't hurt, there was barely any force behind it, but it startles him and makes him tense up. Renee runs a hand through his hair and waits until he's relaxed to hit him again.

"Harder," he says.

"I know what you need."

She hits him again with the exact same amount of force, and he doesn't know if she's making a point, but even if she isn't, it's a reminder to trust her. He told her what he wants out of tonight, and she'll make sure he gets it.

She hits him again, the dull thud of the brush when it hits his skin a mirror to the way it feels. It's a muted pain, the kind that's present and solid but doesn't grab his attention. Sometimes he wants a sharper pain, something that demands his attention with each strike, but with his brush, he can sink into the hits. He allows the heat to spread across his skin until he's pleasantly warm.

Rather than pulling him out of his building headspace, each strike drags him further down.

By the time Renee pauses and runs a hand through his hair, he's breathing heavily, but his eyes are closed. He's exactly where he wants to be, and he turns his head, eyes slitting open as if to ask *What are you doing?*

"Am I putting you to sleep?" she asks.

"No. It's good. I feel really good."

His eyes want to drag closed again but not to sleep. He wants to give himself completely over to what he's feeling, and it's easier when he can't see.

"You look it," Renee tells him. She keeps one hand in his hair and the other palms his ass, her hand cool against his skin. "Are you ready for part two?"

"Yeah."

He doesn't remember what part two is until the brush bristles first scrape against his ass. *Oh,* he thinks then. *Maybe Renee was right.*

Maybe I was falling asleep because I feel awake now. The pain had been a steady pulse under his skin before, but now he can feel every single bristle as it drags against his skin.

"Yes," he says, breath hissing out between his teeth.

"It feels good?" Renee asks, smug because she already knows his answer.

"Yeah."

His ass prickles in the wake of the bristles, and he clings to the feeling of *feeling* and lets it wash over him. He's panting now, curling his fingers into his comforter. He wants more. He wants her fingers digging into his flesh. He wants her hitting him again. He wants—

"Oh," he says, breath knocked out of him when Renee curls her hand around his cock. "I'm hard."

Renee laughs, not mean, but not entirely nice, either. "You are." She leans over him, the denim of her jeans pressed against his ass, her mouth right by his ear. He feels covered, shielded, and his cock jerks in her hand. It feels good, so he rolls his hips into her grip. She allows him to do it the first time, then a second, but on the third, she squeezes him too hard to feel good.

"I'm going to ride you," she reminds him. She strokes his cock again, and between her body pressed against his back and the hand on his cock he thinks he might be able to come. "I'm not sure it'll be any fun for me to ride a soft dick. What do you think?"

Kyle groans as Renee tugs at his earlobe with her teeth, a sharp pain sparking through him even as her thumb sweeps over the tip of his cock.

"I think," he says, struggling to pull in enough air to speak, "that if you keep doing that, then it'll be a moot point."

Renee laughs again, low and dirty, right next to his ear, nothing nice about it this time. "Where's that restraint of yours? Are you really this easy?"

"Fuck." He squeezes his eyes shut. He rocks forward into the tight grip of her hand then back so his ass drags across the rough denim of her jeans. It feels too good to stop, but he knows if he doesn't stop, he'll come. He doesn't want to disappoint Renee, but he can't do this on his own.

"Please," he begs.

She leans even more of her weight on him until his face and his chest are pressed against the bed. "Please what?"

"Please don't let me come like this. Please let me be good for you. It feels so good right now, but it'll feel better when you fuck me."

Renee squeezes his cock once more before she pulls back. A chill runs down his spine once she isn't pressed against him.

"Lie down on your back in the middle of the bed," Renee tells him, "and keep talking."

Kyle scrambles to do as he's told. Somehow, he forgot about his earlier spanking, and he sucks in a breath as his ass drags against his comforter. He wiggles a bit to wake the pain up even more.

"I haven't given you enough?" Renee asks.

"Just want to remember everything you've given me." He props himself up on his elbows so he can watch as she undresses. "I'm glad I went home with you tonight," Kyle says as Renee pulls her shirt over her head.

He groans when he sees her bra, one edged with lace and that pushes her breasts up and close together. He squirms on the bed again as he wonders if she'll let him bury his face in her cleavage and kiss and worship her skin until she has to pull him off with a sharp tug of his hair.

"It's going to feel so good when you fuck me," he says. "I love it when you use me. Love it when you make me desperate."

"You're desperate for me?"

"Yes," he answers, even though it's obvious. His face is flushed and his hair is damp with sweat. His cock is hard and his legs tremble with the effort to keep still. "You love me this way, though. You like to rile me up, to bring me to edge of my control so you have an excuse to hold me down."

"Kyle," she says, condescension dripping from her voice, "I don't need an excuse to hold you down. I can do it because I want to."

She can hold him down with a tight grip on his wrists or with her fingernails digging into his shoulders or even with a soft word and softer touch.

"Please hurry," he tells her, hands clenching in his comforter because he's afraid to touch his cock.

"Touch yourself." Renee lifts her first boot onto the bed. She waits until he wraps his fist around his length to drag the zipper down. "Because you're right. I do love you desperate."

Kyle groans and tugs on his balls so he doesn't come on the spot. Renee grins and tosses her boot on the floor. He feels a flutter of disappointment. He knew she had to take them off to pull her jeans off, but he was hoping she'd wear them again. He likes how she's taller than him in them, likes the press of the heel when they dig into his skin.

"Are you staying the night?" he asks. "Because I want to eat you out tomorrow morning."

It's easy to imagine, her in her boots and nothing else, towering over him while he's on his knees. He wants her hands, insistent in his hair as she pulls his face where she needs it.

"We can probably make that happen." Renee tosses her second boot over her shoulder as if it doesn't matter to her either way.

Kyle squeezes his cock, desperate and wanting and about two seconds away from coming out of his skin. "Are you taking your pants off now? I've been patient, right?"

"You wouldn't know the meaning of the word," Renee tells him, "but you've been good."

She unbuttons her jeans then unzips them so she can tug them and her underwear off together.

"Multitasking," Kyle says. "May I get a condom?"

"You may. You may even put it on."

Kyle flushes as she gives him permission like he *needs* it. He fumbles with the condom as he pulls it out of her drawer, but he doesn't have any problems rolling it on.

Renee climbs onto the bed and straddles him, wearing nothing but her bra now. She stays up on her knees so they aren't touching and Kyle squirms but doesn't try to take more than he's given. She plants one hand near his head, still not touching him, and leans down to kiss him.

He eagerly kisses her back because it's the first time they've touched in too long and because it's something to focus on besides the pain in his ass and the hardness of his cock. He tips his head back and gives her complete control of the kiss.

She nips at his bottom lip and gasps, and Kyle glances down to see her free hand between her legs.

"I can do that," he offers.

"You could, but I don't want your fingers. The only thing you have I'm interested in is your dick."

Humiliation and arousal sweep through him and leave him panting. He forgets sometimes how well she knows him.

"Am I wrong?" Renee asks. She presses soft kisses against the corner of his mouth, across the curve of his cheekbone. "Would your fingers feel better than mine?"

"No," he answers, nearly a whisper, and he knows he's edging into bad territory. Light humiliation is good, but he doesn't want to feel as though he isn't good enough.

Renee kisses him once more on the lips before rising to her knees again. When she pulls her fingers out from between her legs, they're slick. Kyle parts his lips, silently begging for a taste. Renee smiles down at him before she rests her two fingers on his bottom lip.

"Is this what you want?"

At his nod, she slides her fingers into his mouth. He can smell her, taste her, then she sinks down on his cock and he can feel her. Every sense he has is overloaded with Renee, and he whines and sucks on her fingers because he's just on the edge of too much of a good thing.

His hips buck up, and Renee presses him down into the mattress and his ass lights up in pain, and he remembers why he wanted this in the first place. He groans around her fingers, and she grins before she rides him at a brutal pace.

"Is this everything you wanted?" she asks.

He nods, even as he glances at her breasts, held tight by her bra, but still bouncing as she fucks him.

"You want to touch my tits?" she asks.

"Please," he begs around her fingers.

"You told me you wanted me to spank you with your brush then ride you. That's what we agreed to. Maybe next time you'll ask for more."

Kyle makes a low pleading sound in the back of his throat, even though he knows it won't matter. He wasn't lying earlier when he said Renee likes him desperate. She likes him wanting. No matter what they negotiate for she'll find something he didn't know he wanted and make him wish for it. And then she'll tell him no.

He likes the way it twists him up inside when she denies him. He likes how at the end of a session with her he'll always have what he needs but not necessarily what he wants. It means there's always something to look forward to for next time.

"Now that I think about it..." She pulls her fingers from his mouth and wipes his spit on his chin. "We didn't agree to that, either."

"Please," Kyle asks again. She likes to tease him, but he can only handle so much. "Let me have them back. Please."

"Yeah?" She grinds down on his cock, and the tight, hot clench of her threatens to send every thought flying out of his head.

"Yeah," he gasps. She looks smug, but both of them can play this game. "I want you inside me when I'm inside you. Please. Let me—"

Renee growls and shoves her fingers back into his mouth. He sucks them hard, as if he's afraid she'll take them away again. Having two points of contact helps keep him from being overwhelmed by either one. It helps him hold himself together as she rocks her hips harder.

He moans around her fingers as she drops her free hand between her legs to bring herself off. He's careful not to bite down and even more careful not to come because she didn't give him permission. But he wants to. He also wants her to sit on his face so he can lick her release from her and then make her come again. He definitely won't be allowed to do that, but his cock throbs at the thought anyway.

He's the one breathing hard as Renee eases off him, his mouth slack around her fingers. She lightly slaps his cheek with them, leaving a wet spot behind.

"You good?" she asks.

He considers being cheeky and turning the question back on her, but then he thinks about how embarrassing it would be to be forced to jerk off in his own bathroom then sleep on his couch because he was sassy with Renee at the wrong time.

"Yeah," he says again.

He hadn't negotiated to be able to come. Does that mean she won't let him? He never fucking thinks ahead enough when he's with Renee.

"You can touch yourself," Renee tells him.

She's kneeling between his legs, her hands on his thighs, and her words hit him in the right place, a perfect mix of embarrassment and arousal.

"Thank you," he says.

He wraps his hand around his cock, and he's still wearing a condom and it's wet and it takes him a moment to realize he's wet from *her*.

"Oh, fuck." He squeezes the base of his cock and he turns wild eyes on Renee. "Please tell me I'm allowed to come."

"You can come," she tells him, no teasing this time.

It only takes three strokes before he spills, filling the condom. He falls back against the bed, gasping when he remembers that he was spanked earlier this evening.

"Fuck," he hisses.

He looks up at Renee, who watches him with a smile. She runs a hand through his sweat-damp hair. "Good night?"

"It's always a good night with you," he says, offering up a sleazy smile. She tugs on his hair. "Brat."

He shrugs. She knows what she's getting into with him.

"Shower and bed," she tells him.

He doesn't want to move, but he definitely wants a shower before bed. Renee slides off the bed first and grins as she reaches behind her for the clasp on her bra. "I'll be naked in the shower whenever you're ready."

"Are you staying the night?" he asks, quickly following her to his bathroom.

"Yes."

"Staying in my bed?"

"Only if I'm the big spoon," she says. "I hate waking up to a half-chubbed dick up against my ass."

Kyle laughs as he turns his shower on. "That's my preferred way to wake up."

Chapter Three

THE NEXT MORNING is almost perfect. It starts with Renee sitting on his face. She isn't wearing the boots, but it's still pretty damn good. He makes breakfast, and they eat breakfast before she leaves.

Kyle showers, jerks off, and even manages to put in three hours of work before Jenny knocks at his door.

He answers in lounge pants and no shirt. It's his apartment; he's allowed to be as dressed or undressed as he wants.

Jenny still makes a face and says, "No one wants to see that," as she brushes past him.

"A lot of people want to see this," Kyle says, but he finds a T-shirt to throw on.

"They do," Jenny acknowledges when Kyle comes back, T-shirt on and smile tamped down.

Kyle pauses in the entrance to his kitchen. He thought Jenny was teasing him, but no, that was a lead-in to a *conversation*.

He crosses the kitchen to his fridge and pulls out the turkey, bacon, and cheese. "Turkey, bacon, and avocado paninis?"

"Yes," Jenny answers. "I was talking to some people last night. You have a lot of stuff set up."

Kyle sets the bacon next to the stove and hunts down his avocado. "I told you that was my plan. Best case scenario, New Guy notices me. Second best scenario, I have a lot of good scenes. It's a win-win."

"His name is Aidan," Jenny says.

Kyle looks up from his avocado. "You *were* talking last night. What else did you learn?"

Jenny grins as she leans on his island counter. "He's a professor of art history. He might actually be interesting to talk to."

After slicing his avocado, Kyle grabs a tomato. He points the knife at Jenny. "That sounds like a dig at previous people I've scened with."

"Justin."

Kyle shrugs, conceding the point. Justin had been dynamite in bed, big enough to hold Kyle down with ease, and he had a sixth sense for when Kyle wanted to be pushed around before they got down to things and when he needed to be fucked as soon as humanly possible.

Unfortunately, long-lasting relationships aren't built on foreplay and sex. They didn't have anything in common outside the bedroom and after one too many awkward dinners where they had nothing to talk about, they called things off. Kyle still scenes with Justin sometimes, but they weren't going anywhere permanent, and that's what Kyle's looking for now.

He'll do short-term contracts and the occasional hook-up, but what he wants is a relationship, something like what Jenny and Charlotte have.

He cuts them two slices of tomato and wraps the rest of it for later. "Do you think Aidan's the kind of art history guy who hates how art has changed in modern times?"

Kyle's met plenty of people who look down their nose at him for graphic design because *using a computer is cheating* or *that's so easy a child could do it.*

"I think that's something you should be asking him and not me," Jenny says.

"Communication? Gross." Kyle grins so Jenny knows he's joking.

He finishes his prep and puts their paninis in the press. Jenny gave him an unending amount of shit when he bought it for himself as an apartment warming present, but it hasn't stopped her from taking full advantage of his panini-making skills.

"Do you know anything else about him?" It's Kyle's turn to lean against the counter. A name is good, and so is a profession, but that's basic intro stuff. He doesn't know any of the important things. Which means he'll have to continue with his plan. Hopefully New—Aidan will notice him sooner rather than later.

"I don't," Jenny answers. "He's not very chatty. I do know he hasn't hooked up with anyone yet. I don't know if he's scoping the place out or what, but he's only been a few times and no one knows any juicy details."

"You *talked*," Kyle says.

"Only the best for you."

"Thanks." Kyle pulls their sandwiches out. "I'm hoping to work a bit more today and hit the gym. What're you up to?"

"I have pictures to go through." She slides off her stool to rummage through his fridge. "The client has shitty taste."

Kyle laughs. "So, they already rejected that pictures you liked best?"

"Yes." She pulls out a bag of grapes. "Now, I have to go through all the shots from the shoot *again*. And then I have to edit them to make them look worse. I don't understand why people don't trust me. I'm the *photographer*. I know what looks good."

Kyle grins and lets the familiar rant carry them through lunch.

Jenny does the dishes because Kyle cooked. Then she sits down at the island again.

"Serious talk time?" Kyle asks.

"Serious talk time. You've never dropped like that with me."

"I make sure I don't. I was distracted last night. That's on me and I'm sorry."

"Thinking about Aidan?"

"Yeah," he says, and it's hard to admit even though they both know it's true.

"I'm not mad at you," Jenny promises. "It just caught me off-guard. I'm sorry for being weird with Renee."

"We've never been in that situation before. It was new and we weren't ready for it. In the future, Renee's cool. Not that there's going to be a next time. I'll be better."

"Aidan wasn't there last night. Sorry."

"It didn't stop it from being a good scene."

Didn't stop you from being good for me.

Jenny smiles, catching his real meaning. "You were right about the rope. The lavender looked good on you. I think I got more compliments on the rope than I got on you."

"Now, you're trying to hurt my feelings."

"Naw, just keeping your ego in check." She pats his cheek. "Good luck with your work project. Charlotte and I are going out so you can't pester me when you're stuck."

"I won't get stuck," Kyle says as Jenny slides off her stool. "And I can always send you obnoxious texts. It's almost as good as knocking on your door until you answer."

"I don't know why we're friends," Jenny says but she kisses his forehead before she heads out.

Kyle takes a selfie and sends it to her with the caption *because I'm a delight.*

He can hear her laugh from the hallway.

KYLE SHOWS UP at Enchanting Encounters for a beer and to do a little recon of his own. As much as he enjoys the gossip mill, he wants a look at Aidan for himself. He's only seen the guy once and the things he knows about him amount to even less than a shoddy Grindr profile.

He needs information.

When he arrives at the bar, he orders a beer from TJ and finds a group of his friends to sit with.

"Woah," Alexa says when Kyle joins them. "Look who's slumming it with us mere mortals."

Kyle casually flips her off. "I was with Renee last night."

"She doesn't play so rough you couldn't set something up tonight," Alexa says, but she makes room so he can sit with them.

Kyle's ass is a little sore, a pleasant way to remind him of a good night. If he wanted he could scene tonight, but he doesn't want to. He wants to enjoy the way his muscles are tight from last night, the way he has to be careful when he sits down. He's not ready to cover Renee's handiwork with someone else's.

"She doesn't play rough with me," he agrees, "but you know me. I want to make sure the next person I scene with has a blank canvas to work with." He waggles his eyebrows and grins when Alexa laughs.

"You are so full of yourself."

"You're just jealous I'm not full of you," he shoots back.

Lou and Rachel, on the other side of the table, roll their eyes.

"That's a terrible line," Rachel says.

Unlike Renee, Rachel does play rough, much rougher than Kyle's into, but he enjoys talking with her. She tends to only have long-term subs, and for a time Kyle considered subbing for her because maybe if he was good enough, then she'd keep him. But one, that's a terrible mindset to approach a relationship with and two, he likes his scenes blood-free.

"But it works for him," Lou complains. "I don't know how you do it."

Kyle grins, loose and easy because Lou walked right into this one. "You could watch sometime if you want pointers."

Lou kicks him under the table, and Kyle laughs before taking a sip of his beer.

"Is that what you're here for?" Alexa asks. "You're trying to set something up? I heard a rumor you've been making the rounds."

And the gossip mill continues to turn.

"I've talked to Jenny and Renee. I wouldn't call that making the rounds."

Does everyone at Enchanting Encounters know he wants Aidan to notice him? Does *Aidan*? He doesn't want this being common knowledge in case it goes poorly. He doesn't even want it being common knowledge if things go well. He has a reputation and feelings to protect.

"Maybe you should talk to some of the guys," Alexa says. "I mean, I won't turn you down if you ask, but it seems like there's a lot of room for miscommunication if you're trying to lure in your guy by subbing for women."

"There's no communication to miss," Rachel says. "Have you even spoken to the guy?"

"I came here to have a good time tonight." Kyle takes another sip of his beer. "I'm not here for relationship advice."

This is exactly why he doesn't want everyone to know his business. He doesn't want to talk about it. He can handle his own shit.

"I've talked to him," Lou says.

Kyle sort of stalked them at the bar during their conversation. He hadn't been close enough to hear what they were talking about, but he wishes he had. What had made Aidan so interested in Lou? And how can Kyle transfer that interest to him?

Kyle's an exhibitionist and, according to some people, a narcissist. He likes having people's attention on him.

He really wants Aidan's attention.

"He's local," Lou says, pleased to know something no one else does. "He's been on loan to a different university for the past two years. He said it was lonely out there, but it was a good thing because he was able to work on a book he's writing. I can't imagine a guy like him is lonely, but I haven't heard of him going home with anyone."

"Maybe he's reacclimating himself to the scene," Rachel says. "Two years is a long time to be away. There's nothing wrong with not wanting to rush into things."

"Oh!" Alexa says. "There he is."

She nudges Kyle but thankfully doesn't point to the bar. Aidan's talking to TJ, too long to only be ordering a drink, and TJ's cheeks flush.

"Charming TJ?" Rachel asks, impressed. "That takes skill."

"You want to say hi?" Alexa nudges him again, scooting him toward the end of the booth.

"Too late," Lou says as Cynthia approaches Aidan at the bar.

Cynthia is sweet and nice and has a way of curving her shoulders which makes her look smaller than she really is. It always makes Doms want to reach out and hold her. She's everything Kyle attempted to be when he was first trying the whole sub thing and trusted the internet to tell him how to act and how to be.

Kyle isn't good at demure or sweet.

He watches as Aidan tucks a strand of Cynthia's hair behind her ear then he turns to TJ, presumably to order a second drink.

"Maybe tonight's the night," Lou says with a nod in the direction of Aidan and Cynthia.

Kyle's stomach plummets at the sight. If Aidan and Cynthia hit it off, then Kyle loses any hope of he and Aidan being a good match. Kyle and Cynthia have almost nothing in common. Kyle is, well, bratty is probably the nicest word for it.

Everyone at his table stares at him, and Kyle wishes no one knew about his interest.

"What?" He takes a nonchalant sip of his beer. "I'm not hurting for partners. If Aidan and Cynthia hit it off then good for them."

He mostly means it. He wants people to be happy, and if Cynthia can make Aidan happy, then he's all for it. Just, he would prefer to be the one making him happy.

"Did you really drop for Jenny last night?" Alexa asks.

Another thing Kyle doesn't want to talk about. "Yes. We talked about it. It's fine."

"Should Charlotte be worried?" Rachel asks.

Kyle glares at her. "That shit's not funny."

"Sorry," Rachel says.

"They've been together forever," Alexa says. "Good for them, but I can't imagine being tied down to one person for the rest of my life."

"You can't imagine being tied down, period," Rachel says.

Kyle grins. "Yeah, from what I can remember, you enjoy doing the tying."

"Fuck you both."

Kyle shoots Rachel a look from underneath his lashes. "I mean, I'd be into it, but I'm not sure about Rachel here."

"That's two terrible jokes," Alexa says, but she's fighting a smile. "One more and I'm kicking you out of the booth."

"That's not very nice."

"You don't like it when I'm nice to you."

Kyle slides closer so he can drop his head onto her shoulder. "Keep talking dirty to me, babe."

She laughs and shoves him hard enough he almost falls out of the booth. "Not your babe."

Kyle settles himself back in the booth and takes another sip of his beer. He has good friends.

KYLE WAS WRONG.

He has *terrible* friends.

"Go talk to him," Rachel says as Alexa gives Kyle another push.

Cynthia and Aidan shared a drink, but Cynthia went downstairs without Aidan, leaving the man at the bar by himself again.

"No," Kyle says, and he grabs onto the table so Alexa can't shove him out of the booth.

Lou swipes Kyle's beer and finishes it in two big swallows. "Huh, your beer is gone. Guess you should go get a new one."

"I'm not going up there," Kyle says, holding his ground. "I'm hanging out with you guys. Besides, Aidan's clearly not in the mood to pick up tonight."

"He's not in the mood for Cynthia," Lou says. "You and Cynthia aren't the same. He didn't have much interest in me outside of some small talk. Maybe that means *you're* his type."

"What's the worst that could happen?" Rachel asks.

Kyle knows she means to be encouraging, but now all he can think of are worst case scenarios. He could approach Aidan and be flat-out rejected while all his friends watch because he knows them and they will watch. He could approach Aidan and the man could be terribly boring; unlikely but possible. They could find out they're not compatible and Kyle would be back to not having anyone he's interested in pursuing.

Honestly, and he won't tell this to anyone, not his friends at the table and not even Jenny or Charlotte, but it's safest for Aidan to be in potential territory. There, Kyle can pin all his hopes and fantasies on him without having reality shatter them.

He can jerk off to the thought of Aidan staring at him as intently as he stared at Lou the other day, and the fantasy won't be ruined by knowing Aidan is an art snob or a jerk.

"Aren't you the one who told me there's no such thing as rejection?" Alexa asks.

"Yeah," Lou chimes in. "You always say it's not rejection, it's just two people with differing interests."

Kyle is known for saying that because he doesn't see the point in getting all twisted up because someone doesn't want to fuck him or scene with him. No matter how attractive a person is, if their interests don't match up with his then no one will have a good time.

Aidan's different, though.

"Oh, shit," Alexa says, her voice quieter as if she's figured it out. "You *like* him."

"Are we back in middle school?" Kyle asks.

"If we are, it's because you started it. Are you seriously *wooing* him with demos?"

"No, I'm doing demos because I like them and Wendy asked me to."

"But if you happen to be noticed then it's a bonus?" Alexa sighs and ruffles his hair. "Sometimes I forget you're as emotionally stunted as the rest of us."

"I am not," Kyle says.

He wants Aidan to approach *him*. It's not his usual style. Normally he's more assertive, but Aidan is different. Kyle wants more than a couple of scenes with Aidan which he needs to hook his interest. If Aidan approaches him once, then he'll keep coming back. Well, that's the theory, anyway.

"I didn't realize it was like that," Alexa says, all teasing gone from her voice. "We'll help you, yeah?"

"Of course, we will," Rachel says.

"It won't matter if Kyle's too chicken shit to talk to him," Lou says. "But, yeah, I guess I'm in."

"When's your next scene?" Rachel braces her arms on the table and leans in like they're laying out a battle plan.

"Next week," Kyle answers.

"I'll make sure Aidan's there," Alexa says. She pulls Kyle in for a sideways hug. "That's what friends are for, right?"

Kyle takes it back. His friends aren't so terrible after all.

Chapter Four

KYLE'S NEXT SCENE is a guided one with Renee and a fledgling Dom named Richard. Kyle wasn't lying when he said he's one of Wanda's favorite subs. He's experienced, and he's open with his thoughts and his feedback, which means he's often tapped to scene with people new to the lifestyle. Or he'll be part of a guided scene to help both inexperienced Doms and subs grow more comfortable.

He's done plenty of scenes like this before, but he's never done one in public. New Doms are paired with a mentor to talk them through everything and to answer any questions as they come up, the same way new subs are paired with a mentor, but often these guided scenes are done in a private room.

He's done guided scenes where Renee or Alexa will put him through his paces while a new Dom watches and learns. He's done scenes where they work together and scenes where the new Dom has the reins and the established Dom is there to make sure nothing goes wrong.

But doing one of these on the main floor is new, and Kyle's skin prickles with anticipation.

He likes new.

He met with Renee and Richard on Wednesday at the coffee shop on the first floor to run through the details again. Richard isn't as new as some of the people Kyle's worked with before, and he wants to branch out into one-on-one scenes without a supervising Dom. This public scene is to make sure he's ready for it and a chance for him to show off to any interested subs in the audience.

Kyle likened it to a coming-of-age ball and earned himself a light slap on the back of the head from Renee.

That's nothing compared to what he'll get today.

He grins and does a little happy dance before he shimmies out of his jeans. He loves a good spanking when it's for play. He doesn't like punishment spankings, which is the whole point, he supposes, but that's not what's on the table for tonight. He'll have Richard's hands on him and Renee's voice, and he can't wait.

He carefully folds his jeans then his T-shirt and puts them in his locker. He's in only his briefs now, but those are for Richard or Renee to take off. They want him covered until he's out of the locker room and where they've set up the scene.

It's different than his scenes with Jenny.

With Jenny, his briefs stay on so the focus will be her work. Tonight, *he's* the focus.

He'll have two sets of hands on him and the attention of an entire room. His grin returns and he finds a mirror to check himself over in before he heads out.

Renee and Richard are set up by a padded table as Renee shows Richard how to adjust the height. Richard's tall. He easily has a couple inches on Renee, even though she's in heels. He's broad too. His T-shirt pulls tight across his shoulders. He's built like someone who spends a couple hours a day in the gym.

Of course, the real question is whether he knows what to do with all those muscles.

There are other people in the playroom, some making use of the club's equipment, others taking advantage of a willing audience, and still others milling around while they wait for something to catch their eye. How many of them are waiting for him?

Even though he's tempted, Kyle doesn't linger as he looks around the room. He doesn't try to pinpoint faces or figure out how many people are here because it's better when he doesn't know. It means later, when his head is bowed and he can't see anything but the table, he can let his imagination run wild. He can fill the room to bursting or he can imagine a small private audience.

He shakes himself out of his thoughts and slinks up to Renee. "Reporting for duty, ma'am."

She flicks his ear. "Have you noticed you only call me ma'am when you're being fresh?"

"Part of my charm." Kyle leans against the table and makes a show of looking Richard over. "Let me guess, by the end of our session, I'll have a craving for Dick?"

Renee grabs his ear and twists it this time, hard enough to hurt. "This is supposed to be a fun spanking, but we can make you cry instead. I'm sure your admirers won't mind. You sound good when you're begging for more, but you look just as good with tears running down your cheeks."

"Sorry," Kyle says. "Will you let my ear go now?"

"Will you behave?"

Kyle nods. He likes to feel out where the lines are before a scene, and tonight it looks like he won't have a lot of leeway to be...himself. *Bratty*, he hears in Renee's voice. If he was in a private room with Renee, then he might push to see what happened if he crossed the line, but he won't do that to Richard.

Richard deserves Kyle at his best. Tonight's a big step for him, the first time he's done a public scene, and his nerves are clearly bad enough without Kyle being difficult.

"Hop on the table," Renee says. "I want to make sure it's the right height."

Kyle dutifully climbs up, and Renee puts a hand on his hip and says, "This is obviously too tall for me, see here? But let's see if it works for you."

Renee likes to hit Kyle while he leans over something. She likes to see how long before his knees buckle and he can't hold himself up anymore. One of his favorite scenes of theirs was when he was braced against the wall as she paddled him, and he had to struggle to stay present enough to keep himself standing when all he wanted was to sink into what she was doing.

He'd broken down in tears by the end.

He smiles at the memory.

"This'll work," Renee says. She taps his ankle. "You can get down now."

Kyle has a few snappy comments about how he can go down whenever he wants and how he's damn good at it, but he holds them back.

Renee runs a hand through his hair, rewarding him for keeping his mouth shut. Kyle tips his head back into the touch and Renee uses her free hand to scratch faint lines down his throat. When he swallows, the press of her fingernails is sharp against his skin.

Being held like this reminds him he's not in control and the sure way she handles him reassures him he doesn't need to be. Renee will take care of him. All he has to do is trust her and do as she says.

His eyes flutter shut, and when they open again, the world around him is softer, less like something he needs to fight and more like something for him to accept.

"Good," Renee tells him.

Yeah, I am good. And I'll continue to be good.

"He's very affectionate," Renee tells Richard, and Kyle has to bite back against a groan because being talked about like this is one of his surefire kinks. It's one of the reasons he's often part of training sessions. There's a lot of talking about him. "He likes being touched. It's a good way to soften him up for a scene."

She moves so she's standing behind Kyle, still holding him with a hand in his hair and another around his neck, but it means Richard has an unobstructed view of Kyle and Kyle has an unobstructed view of Richard.

Kyle has to tilt his head up to look at him.

He licks his lips.

Renee pinches the thin skin of his neck.

"You can't even see what I'm doing," Kyle says.

"But I know you." She rubs the sting out of the spot she pinched. "You don't need to seduce him. He's already a sure thing."

"Maybe I want him to like me." Kyle flutters his eyelashes. He has to fight his smile. "You like me, Richard?"

Richard relaxes at the teasing, which is exactly what Kyle was aiming for. Kyle wants tonight to be a good experience for Richard which means it should be fun.

"I think I'll like you better once you're naked," Richard says.

"Most people do. You can undress me if you want."

Richard steps closer, and Kyle has to tilt his head back even more to keep looking at Richard's face. It makes something hot coil in his gut as Richard takes another step closer so Kyle's trapped between him and Renee. He likes feeling outsized and outmatched by his partners. They don't have to be bigger than him—he's subbed for plenty of people who make him go to his knees with just a look or change in their tone—but it doesn't hurt when they're built like Richard.

Richard snaps the waistband of Kyle's briefs against his skin, not hard enough to hurt, just a sting that forces Kyle to focus.

"I want you paying attention," Richard says. He hooks his fingers through the elastic waistband, but he doesn't show any signs of stripping Kyle anytime soon.

"I am," Kyle promises. He's not sure whether to look at Richard's face or the curl of his fingers or to see if Richard's hard in his jeans. He's spoiled for choice, and it makes him want even more. It makes him want to say thank you however Richard asks him to.

Richard eases Kyle's waistband down until his briefs are at his knees. "Take them the rest of the way off," Richard says and catches Kyle's hands in his.

Kyle looks at his wrists, small in the circle of Richard's fingers, and has to take a deep breath before he can do anything else. *This is a demo, I need to keep a clear-ish head. This isn't about me having a good time. It's about helping him.*

"He wants a show," Renee whispers in Kyle's ear, reminding him there are people besides him and Richard here.

He grounds himself with her voice and her hands, now on his waist. He takes another breath before he pulls his left foot up and hooks his socked toes through his right leg hole. He tugs his briefs down, an awkward stretch of material. His knee knocks against Richard's thigh, and Renee holds him steady, and he's caught between them, *held* between them.

When he finally steps out of his briefs, he's breathing heavily and he's trembling, and they haven't even begun yet.

Richard puts two fingers under Kyle's chin and tilts his head up.

"I think I have your attention now," Richard says.

Kyle nods, throat too dry to speak. He has a tendency to dare Doms to prove themselves to him—he won't go to his knees for just anyone— and sometimes it doesn't work out. Not everyone wants a sub who's pushy, but other times it works out really well.

Tonight is one of those nights.

Kyle stares up at Richard and lets him see the flush in Kyle's cheeks and the spark in his eyes, and how everything so far is really doing it for him. Richard's handling him well, and he deserves to know it.

He'll be popular here. He'll make a lot of subs very happy.

"I'm going to put you on the table," Richard says.

He hesitates just a moment to give Kyle a chance to say no, and when Kyle doesn't protest, Renee drops her hands away so Richard can lift him and set him down on the table.

"That's hot," Kyle says. "Can I kiss you?"

"No."

Kyle huffs. "So that's how it's gonna be? Wham, bam." He makes a slapping motion with his hand. "Thank you, *sir*?"

Richard's learning because he just grins. "Are you worried I won't hit you hard enough if you don't rile me up?" He steps between Kyle's legs, moves into Kyle's space until there's only inches between them. "I'm going to take care of you just fine."

Kyle's dick jumps at the promise, and he can't find it in him to be embarrassed. Confidence is hot, and so is the way Richard palms his thighs.

"Let's get started," Richard says.

Kyle's completely on board with this plan. The sooner they start, the sooner Richard can make him feel good and the sooner Kyle can jerk off in his apartment. They haven't even gotten to the good stuff yet, and Kyle already has a number of things to get himself off with.

He tries to turn over, but Richard's hands press down on his thighs, holding him in place.

Kyle glances up at Richard, and the man's eyes are dark and focused, some of the earlier teasing gone. He's serious now, and Kyle responds to the change, going loose under Richard's touch.

"May I turn over?" Kyle asks.

Richard smiles and brushes his lips over Kyle's, too quick to be called a kiss. "You may."

It takes Kyle a moment to collect himself, and Richard steps back so Kyle can move to his hands and knees. He drops to his elbows and lifts his ass in the air, grinning when he hears Richard's sharp intake of breath. Richard isn't the only one who knows how to leverage what he's got.

"He takes good care of himself," Renee says. "He's vain that way."

Kyle opens his mouth to defend himself, but Renee puts two fingers under his chin to close his jaw. Kyle squeezes his eyes shut and reminds himself he's supposed to be easy for them.

Richard's hands cover Kyle's ass, mapping out the places he's going to mark. Or maybe he just wants to touch. Kyle trembles, but doesn't push back into the touch. Richard might let him get away with it, but Renee would call him greedy and tell Richard to stop touching.

"You're lucky," Renee says. "Not every sub wants to be displayed like this in front of a crowd."

She's talking to Richard, but the words are for Kyle, and they allow him to relax. Richard *is* lucky because Kyle's a good sub. And he'll prove it by being good for Richard. Renee's here to make sure everyone has what they want by the end, which means Kyle doesn't need to push. Even if Richard is new and doesn't pick up on all Kyle's cues, Renee will.

"There you go," Renee praises. She runs a hand through Kyle's hair. When she addresses Richard, her voice is more clinical. "Touch his sides."

Richard does, sliding his hands up Kyle's back then around until his fingertips reach for Kyle's stomach.

"Feel how he's tense?" Renee asks. "He's excited for tonight, but anticipation can be just as bad as nerves when it comes to a sub tightening up. You need him relaxed before you can start or it won't be enjoyable for anyone involved."

Kyle knows Renee's explaining important things Richard needs to know, but it feels as though she's scolding him. She shouldn't have had to explain because Kyle knows better. *Is* better.

He takes a deep breath and releases his tension as he exhales. He relaxes between the two of them and is rewarded with Richard's soft, "Wow."

"Some subs can relax with a reminder," Renee says. "Some need a little more coaxing." Her hand runs through Kyle's hair again. "This is Kyle's weak spot. Give him a scalp massage, and he'll melt."

Renee slips her hand from his hair as she steps back, and Kyle knows this is a sign she's passing control over to Richard. She might offer a bit of advice or step in if she needs to, but for now, this is Richard's show.

Without meaning to, Kyle braces himself for the first blow, but instead, Richard's hands sweep up his back then back down like he wants to touch as much of Kyle's skin as he can. Kyle arches into the touch, pushing back everywhere Richard's hands touch, searching for more.

"You like that," Richard says.

It isn't a question, but Kyle answers, anyway. "You feel good."

"Hmm." Richard skims his hands over Kyle's ass and touches his thighs. Kyle works out for fitness and to make his body an asset when he picks up. He doesn't work out for bulk, isn't looking for big muscles, but he still feels cheated at how much skin Richard's hands can cover.

It makes Kyle feel small in the best way possible, and he blows out an unsteady breath.

It catches him off-guard when Richard brings a hand down on his ass, and his breath catches in his throat before it escapes in a low groan. His skin tingles where it was struck, a reminder of what just happened and a promise of more, and Kyle groans again because this is exactly what he's waited patiently for.

"Does that feel good too?" Richard asks, a smugness to his voice which says Kyle doesn't need to bother answering.

Kyle finds cocky hotter than he should. "Do it again and find out."

Richard laughs and runs his fingers over where he laid the first hit. Is Kyle's skin already pink? Can Richard trace where he left his mark? How long will it take for Kyle to stay pink for the rest of the night?

The next blow also catches him off guard, as if between the first hit and a gentle touch Kyle forgot why he was here. He hisses a breath out through his teeth and tilts his hips up, wanting more.

Richard obliges.

Somehow, Kyle always forgets how good someone's hand on his ass feels. It means he can experience the sensation almost like it's new every time; the initial shock when the first blow lands then the need for more and more until he's had his fill.

He whines when Richard stops spanking him. The hand braced on Kyle's hip gives him a squeeze.

"That was just the warm-up," Richard says. "I'm not done."

"Good."

"Are you feeling warmed up?" Richard presses the backs of his hands to Kyle's ass, and they aren't cold, but they're cooler than Kyle's skin. "You feel warm."

A moment later, Kyle feels the press of smoother skin against his ass. Richard's *cheek*. "Fuck," Kyle groans.

"Renee told me you were vocal," Richard says as he spreads his hands across Kyle's ass again, touching as much skin as he can.

Kyle hopes that won't be a problem. He can keep his mouth shut if he needs to, but he likes to be loud. He likes his Dom to know how he's feeling because subs aren't the only ones who deserve praise and recognition. And because scenes often require him to stay still, it's easier to keep his body contained if he can run his mouth.

"You're ready for the main event," Richard says. He squeezes Kyle's ass, fingers pressing into Kyle's skin, keeping the pain awake so he can build on it. "Here's the deal. I'll only spank you if you tell me how much you like it.

Once you stop, I stop. I don't want to do anything you don't like."

Fuck. Kyle's cock throbs between his legs, a reminder that he's hard and that Richard is pushing all the right buttons. He doesn't know if Richard's tapping into his desire to be loud or he likes being asked for things or if he's actually concerned about doing something Kyle doesn't want. No matter the reason, this is doing it for him.

Richard cards his hand through Kyle's hair, and Kyle melts into the touch just in time for Richard to tighten his grip and lift Kyle's head up. "Deal?" Richard asks.

"Deal," Kyle says, dizzy. Then Richard pushes his head back down, and Kyle bites his wrist as he groans again.

Kyle bows his head, his breathing loud and raspy to his ears and a steady pulse of arousal low in his belly, and he's ready for this to really start. For a moment, nothing happens, then he remembers Richard's words and *oh.*

"You warmed me up," Kyle says. "Are you gonna show me what you got?"

Richard flicks Kyle's ear, something he picked up from Renee.

"Fuck, fine," Kyle says. "Spank me again. Please."

"All you had to do was ask." Richard brings his hand down on Kyle's skin, the crack louder than the pain. Kyle wants more.

"Harder. I know I'm not built like you, but I'm not fragile."

Richard lands his next hit in the exact same place, with the exact same force behind it. "I told you to tell me how much you like it not how you want it."

"I like it. I like your hands on me. Like—" His thoughts scatter when Richard's hand comes down again, this time with more bite. "I like how you keep me guessing." He shudders as Richard lands two blows in quick succession then waits a full count of ten before landing the next one.

"I like the sting of it, and I like how before the pain can settle you hit me again."

The longer the spanking goes on, the more derailed Kyle's thoughts become. Instead of feedback he says things like *yes* and *so good* and *please don't stop.* After a while, he loses even those words.

His ass is on fire, but each smack of Richard's hand builds Kyle toward something. A few more blows, and he could come. A few more and he'll cry. A few more and he'll slip down and down and down until someone pulls him up again.

In the back of his mind, he knows he isn't here for any of those, but it's hard to remember with pleasure humming through his body. He *wants* and what he wants is right within his grasp. A little more and—

Richard rubs his hands over Kyle's ass, somehow soothing and aggravating his skin at the same time. Maybe if Richard drags his nails down Kyle's skin...

"Please," Kyle begs. His lashes are damp when he blinks, and he needs more. He doesn't even care what, as long as this feeling doesn't fade. "You feel so good. Don't stop."

"Shh." Richard slides his hands into Kyle's hair which is cheating because Kyle tips his head into the touch and loses his train of thought. "You did good. Your ass is so pink. I want to see how long it'll last."

There's an idea. Kyle twists so he's looking up at Richard, somehow on his knees. Like this, their faces almost touch. It would be easy to lean in and kiss him. Maybe afterward Richard will lay Kyle out in bed and trail his big hands up and down Kyle's skin, telling him how good he was and staring at the work he did on Kyle's ass.

Kyle sinks down on his heels and gasps when it awakens the fire in his ass. *Even better idea, blow Richard on my knees like his. Cock in my mouth and pain in my ass.*

"Hey," Renee says, demanding Kyle's attention.

Kyle turns toward the sound as much as he's able with Richard's hands still in his hair. He gives Renee a slow once-over and wonders if it would be better to be on his knees with Renee standing over him. She knows what he likes. She'd grip his hair hard and—

"We're not done yet," Renee says.

"Mmm." Kyle pushes into Richard's touch as he licks his lips. "Like the way that sounds."

"Oh, Kyle." She shakes her head. "Come on, both of you."

Kyle slides off the table, and Richard wraps his arm tight around Kyle's shoulders. Kyle doesn't need the support, but he doesn't turn down the touch. He likes the way Richard pulls him against his side as if he's something precious to hold onto. Or maybe as if he doesn't want to lose Kyle quite yet.

Not going anywhere. Kyle slips his hand under Richard's shirt. *We're not done yet, Renee promised. Maybe I can convince Richard to lose the shirt.*

"We'll do our initial talk here," Renee says. "We'll do a more extensive one in a day or two, but this is a good place to begin."

Kyle's only half-listening because he has more important things to focus on, like getting even closer to Richard. His ass feels ten degrees hotter than the rest of him which makes him shiver. He wants a hug, wants someone pressed up against him. Maybe Richard will fuck him while he's on his stomach, blanket him with that big body and keep Kyle warm. Maybe they'll cuddle. He could go for either right now.

"Not one of the rooms?" Richard asks, confused. It strikes a note of discord in Kyle's brain. Richard was in control and now he's not, and that's not right. It— "What about aftercare?"

"We'll still do it, but in here," Renee promises.

Kyle drags his gaze away from Richard to look around. He'd recognize the green lockers lining the wall anywhere. Kyle has a locker here, and he knew this was where they'd go after the scene, but he'd gotten caught up, and it makes his return to reality more abrupt than he'd anticipated.

"Ugh." He looks down at his cock, still hard from the spanking, and sighs.

There's no sex allowed in the locker rooms. There are private rooms for people who want orgasms, and there is certain allowance made in some of the public areas, but there's none in the locker room which means Kyle isn't going to his knees for anyone.

"You know the rules," Renee says.

"Yeah," Kyle says. And because he doesn't think he should be the only one suffering, he looks over his shoulder at Richard and adds, "Shame because I look real fucking pretty when I come."

Renee barks out a laugh as Richard draws in a short gasp and stares at Kyle as if he's thinking about it.

"It won't kill you to wait." Renee pulls some cream out of her locker. "It might even make it better when you get off later."

"Really?" Richard asks, catching the cream when Renee tosses it to him. "You'll think about this later?"

"Don't grow bashful on me now," Kyle says. He reaches up to pat Richard's cheek. "You're hot when you believe in yourself. And yes, I'm definitely thinking about you when I jerk off tonight. I like being spanked, and I really liked you doing the spanking."

"Cool." Richard flicks open the cap on the cream. "Bend over the bench."

"I've seen this porno," Kyle says as he bends over.

"I liked you better begging."

"You'd like me even better on my knees," Kyle says as Richard rubs the cream into his ass. "Is that what you'll jerk off to tonight? Me on my knees for you, thanking you for taking care of me so well?"

Richard's fingers pause. "Well, I will be *now*."

Kyle smirks. "It's what I was hoping for when Renee told us we weren't done. And then she dragged us in here."

"Sure," Renee says, "Make *me* the bad guy. You know the rules."

"Yeah."

Richard finishes rubbing the cream into Kyle's skin. "Should we do anything else? Ice?"

"I'm good," Kyle says. He straightens up and takes inventory of his body. He's a little stiff from being in one position, his ass is sore, but nothing bad or unexpected. He rubs a hand over his ass and grins because he'll have to sleep on his stomach tonight. "I'm really good. Missing some clothes, though."

Renee opens his locker and tosses him his clothes. He isn't expecting it, and they hit him in the chest then fall to the ground.

"Huh," Kyle says.

"So, we don't need to cuddle or anything?" Richard asks. He picks Kyle's clothes up for him and sets them on the bench.

"Not after a demo spanking. I mean, I won't turn you down if you want to, but it's not something I need."

"I'm good. I just feel like I should do more."

"You could help me with my clothes," Kyle says. Now that he's out of the scene and remembers the plan for the night, he's in a better headspace, but he'll never turn down someone's hands on him.

"Sure."

Richard pulls Kyle's briefs out of his back pocket which probably shouldn't be attractive, but it hits Kyle solidly in the chest. His earlier arousal comes back in full force, and he'd sit down, but he's still bare-assed.

"Renee, tell me I'm not allowed to fuck Richard in the locker room," Kyle says, even as he eyes Richard then the surrounding walls as if he's looking for the best one to use.

"You're not allowed to fuck Richard in the locker room," she dutifully tells him.

"Really?" Richard asks as he hands Kyle's briefs to him. He frowns a little, eyebrows pulling together in suspicion. "You're not trying to inflate my ego, are you? You're a big deal, and I'm new at this."

Kyle tugs on his briefs without any teasing and fixes Richard with his most serious look of the night. "This isn't empty flattery, I'm not into that. It makes it so people don't trust you. I enjoyed what we did. Rationally, I know we only agreed on a spanking, and it was all we should've agreed on since it was your first public scene, but it doesn't stop me from wanting more. This—" he pats the bulge of his dick "—doesn't always appreciate rationality."

Richard laughs a little.

Kyle hands him his jeans and makes him hold them as he steps into them. He makes Richard help him pull his shirt on too.

"You're spoiled," Renee says.

"I'm a treasure and I deserve to be cherished."

Clothes on, Kyle feels more grounded, and it means he's prepared for Renee to hold up a yellow bracelet.

"This is the more important part of doing a scene at the club," she tells Richard as he takes it from her. "It means no one can buy Kyle an alcoholic drink and no one can take him home for the night or do another scene with him here."

Kyle holds his wrist out so Richard can fasten the bracelet. "It's to keep me from making bad decisions when I'm floating on endorphins or too deep in subspace."

"Which you're not right now," Richard says.

"Which I'm not," Kyle confirms. He glances over his shoulder at Renee. "I'm sure you two have more chitchatting to do. It's time for me to have my juice."

"Mingle on your way to the bar," Renee tells him. "You had a big audience, let them tell you how good you were."

Kyle grins because she knows what he likes. "Are you gonna be the first?"

"Brat."

Kyle blows her a kiss and brushes his lips across Richard's cheek. "We'll talk more over coffee. Take a day or two to figure out how you felt about the scene before we dissect it."

"Okay." Richard shoves his hands into his pockets. "You'll be fine on your own?"

"I won't be on my own. Didn't you hear Renee? I have an adoring public waiting for me."

"Get out." Renee laughs. "This locker room isn't big enough for your ego."

Chapter Five

KYLE SAUNTERS OUT of the locker room with a grin on his face and a bounce in his step and he winks at the first person he catches looking.

"I can't believe Renee unleashed you on us," Rachel says.

Kyle waggles his eyebrows. "Are you saying you want to leash me? I didn't think you were into that but—" He breaks off laughing when Rachel smacks his shoulder.

"Don't you have a cranberry juice to drink?"

"Renee was very specific. She said *you had a big audience. Let them tell you you did a good job.*" He slants another look at Rachel, this one expectant.

She huffs, fond and exasperated, as she ruffles his hair. "You did a good job. I'm disappointed it ended when it did. I love it when you cry."

Kyle's warmed with the praise and he pushes into her touch like an overgrown cat. "You say the nicest things to me."

Rachel presses a kiss to his forehead. "Give me a call later if you want to cry."

"I'll think about it," he promises before he continues toward the bar.

He's stopped by a few friends and a few familiar faces, people who want to touch his arms or his shoulders and tell him he did good. One guy wants to know Kyle's gym routine which is flattering if also unexpected.

They exchange weightlifting tips then he heads upstairs to the bar where he spots Cynthia.

She and Lou have their heads bent together, whispering about something, but Kyle doesn't hesitate to interrupt, throwing an arm around their shoulders once he's close enough.

"Hey," Kyle says.

"You're perky," Lou tells him.

"Part of my natural charm."

"He just came from a scene," Cynthia explains.

"Part of your ongoing plan?"

"Mmm." Kyle rubs his face against Lou's neck. "He offered to cuddle me after. It was sweet."

"And yet you're nuzzling *me*."

"Maybe you smell better." Kyle sniffs Lou's neck. "Huh. New aftershave?"

"No," Lou says and tries to wiggle out of Kyle's grasp.

"Did you come from a scene of your own?"

"What?" Cynthia asks. "Really?"

"It wasn't a scene," Lou mumbles.

Kyle's arm goes slack with surprise. "Did you come here from a *date*?"

"Oh, wow," Cynthia says.

Lou, bright red now, tries to scowl. "It's not a big deal."

"Of course, it's a big deal. Since when are you going steady with someone?"

"It's not like that." Lou looks miserable enough that Kyle stops teasing.

"Sorry," Kyle says.

Lou shrugs. "Just someone I work with. She's really nice, but she isn't part of the scene, and that never goes well. Either she'll find out what I'm into and think it's weird or she'll say it's okay with me doing non-sexual scenes at the club and then change her mind and then we'll have a big blow-up fight and—"

"Hey," Kyle interrupts because no one should look sad after going on a date with someone they like. "There are other ways for it to play out. Maybe she's into the scene and you don't know it. Maybe she'll be into it once she's introduced. I swear I'm not hitting on you, but you're breathtaking up on the St. Andrew's Cross. And even if she doesn't want to be the one to wield your instrument of choice for the night, I can't imagine she'd turn down watching. I watch you get your ass beat all the time, and I'm not even into you."

"You're terrible at this," Lou says.

"I tried."

"You did," Cynthia says. She pats his arm. "But let me take over from here?"

"Probably for the best."

"Let me mope, you have your man to pursue," Lou says, and he points to the bar where Aidan's lounging on one of the stools.

The man's in khakis and a plaid button-up which is clearly a sign of how far gone Kyle is because khakis don't look good on anyone, and Kyle's still stupidly into him.

"He's not my man," Kyle says, but he can't tear his eyes away. Had Aidan been here for the show? Did he see Kyle up on the table? Did he wish he was in Richard's place? Did he see the way Kyle's ass turned pink and hear how much Kyle loved it and feel a frisson of want?

"Certainly not if you stand here drooling. Go, try speaking words. Maybe you'll get a scene out of it."

Kyle presses a sloppy kiss to his cheek. "Things will work out for you," he promises.

Kyle's three steps closer to the bar when he wonders if this is such a good idea. He likes having crushes. He enjoys the quiver of anticipation when he sees someone he's interested in; likes to work himself into knots over whether they're interested in him back. What if Aidan isn't as interesting as Kyle's built him up to be? What if he is, but doesn't return Kyle's interest?

Then he continues living his life the way he was before Aidan.

Boring answer, but ultimately true. And until he talks to Aidan, he'll be caught in uncertain limbo.

Kyle takes a fortifying breath, and then he approaches Aidan. *This is what I wanted*, he reminds himself. This is his opportunity to talk to Aidan and figure out if there's anything there besides surface level attraction.

Maybe, in his fantasies, Aidan swept Kyle off his feet like some kind of fairytale Dom, but real life isn't like that.

Kyle drops onto the stool next to Aidan and smiles when Aidan glances over at him. "Buy me a drink?"

Aidan's eyes, a light brown, dip down to the yellow bracelet on Kyle's wrist.

Kyle's smile grows. "Cranberry juice. Only wholesome fun allowed for me for the rest of the night."

"Sounds like a hardship," Aidan says, his voice deeper than Kyle expected. It's raspy, as if he's been talking all day.

Since he's a professor, it's entirely possible he has spent all day talking. Kyle isn't the only one who could use a drink, it looks like.

"We all have our burdens to bear," Kyle says.

TJ comes over, a flush on his cheeks because it's a busy night and he has to run from one end of the bar to the other. It makes his curls plaster to his forehead. It's cute in a sloppy sort of way, and Kyle turns his smile on his favorite bartender.

"Did you shrink your shirts in the wash again or have you been working out?"

"What do you mean, again?"

Kyle sighs. "I was trying to flirt."

"Oh, is that what that was?" TJ laughs. "You're in a good mood tonight."

Kyle flashes his yellow bracelet.

"Cranberry juice?"

"Aren't you supposed to lean on the bar and ask me if I want my usual in a sultry voice? I feel cheated."

TJ lifts his eyebrows.

"Cranberry juice, please."

"Good scene?" TJ asks before he turns to pour Kyle's drink.

"Yeah. Training session with Renee and Richard."

"I wouldn't expect that pair," TJ says.

"Worked out well for me."

"Doesn't everything?" He sets Kyle's drink on the counter. "Things are busy tonight, but I'll try and swing by later."

"For details?" Kyle asks. "We both know this is my only drink."

TJ's glance at Aidan isn't even close to subtle. "Details, sure." Then he *winks* and moves on to the woman flagging him down.

Kyle groans and wonders if he should leave the club and never return. "Can we pretend you didn't just see that?"

"If you want," Aidan says. "Should I also pretend I didn't watch you earlier tonight?"

"The point of public scenes is for people to watch." Kyle turns to Aidan with bravery he doesn't feel. This is exactly what he was aiming for—Aidan to catch a glimpse of him in his element—but now he's nervous. What if Aidan didn't like it? Didn't like *him*?

"You seem to thrive with an audience."

"I like being watched." Kyle takes a sip of his drink. "But one person's attention can be as potent as a whole crowd's."

Aidan hums and takes a drink of his beer. His fingers curl around the bottle as he lifts it, and Kyle imagines those same fingers curled around his wrist. Would Aidan be gentle? Would he reel Kyle in or would his grip be tighter, something that might leave bruises, a reminder that Kyle's been caught?

Aidan clears his throat, and Kyle flushes as he realizes he's been staring.

He's usually smoother than this. But apparently, tonight is not a night for smoothness or subtlety, so he leans against the bar and asks, "Did you enjoy the show?"

Aidan's lips curve up in a smile. "I enjoyed you," he says, casual, as if he doesn't understand how he can devastate Kyle with just three words.

Kyle bites his bottom lip to keep from pressing for more, and Aidan's hand twitches like he wants to reach out and touch, but knows he isn't allowed. Kyle slowly releases his lip and wraps his hands around his glass so he doesn't fidget. Aidan's attention is just as intense as he hoped it would be. Just a look and a couple of words and Kyle wants to sway closer or slip from his stool and kneel at Aidan's side.

But he has a yellow bracelet on his wrist and the marks of another Dom on his ass which means he's off limits, no matter how badly he wishes it was different.

"That wasn't a yes," Kyle says.

He needs to think about something besides where this night could go if Kyle was free.

"Perceptive," Aidan says, and it sounds like a compliment. Kyle ducks his head so Aidan won't see him blush. "You thrive with an audience, but I struggle being a part of one. I see things I would do differently or better and they irritate me."

He wants to press and find out what Aidan would do differently if he had Kyle naked before him, but he's not sure he'd be able to handle it, and it's unfair to Richard.

"Too much professor in you?"

Aidan looks surprised, a flash of unguarded emotion, before he smiles. "Yes."

"You've been the talk of the club. I was actually hoping you'd be part of the crowd tonight."

The surprise returns, and it takes Aidan longer to recover this time. "Oh?"

Kyle shrugs, aiming for unaffected. "I wanted to make sure we had something to talk about before I approached you the first time."

I wanted to see if you'd approach me first. I still wish you had, but I don't have the patience for a long game.

"You wanted my attention," Aidan says. "Now that you have it, what's your next step?"

"Ask you for coffee and see if you want an opportunity to, uh, enjoy me in a more hands-on situation."

Kyle wants to pull his lip between his teeth again, his favorite nervous habit, but he remembers how Aidan didn't like it. He drops his gaze to the table instead before chancing a look up.

"I wasn't able to buy you a drink tonight," Aidan says. "I'd like to buy you a coffee."

"I'd like that too," Kyle says. Then because he's always pushing, he adds, "Maybe you could tell me how you'd approach a scene."

"Over coffee?"

"Or now. I wouldn't mind having something to think about when I'm at home later."

Aidan smiles, and Kyle's seen enough smiles to know this one means he won't get what he wants. It's the kind of smile that says Aidan's amused by Kyle but will turn him down, anyway. Kyle hates how he's a little turned on by it.

"You have plenty to think about," Aidan tells him. "And when you think about me, I don't want it to be with the evidence of someone else's hands on you."

Well, fuck. Kyle squirms on his stool. "Are you telling me not to jerk off to you tonight?"

"Yes," Aidan says, his voice rumbling across Kyle's skin. "That's exactly what I'm telling you."

Kyle fiddles with his drink, wondering how far he can push this. Because he's him, the answer is always farther. "So you'd rather I think about someone else?"

Aidan's eyes narrow, a dozen answers flitting across his face, but then his gaze catches on Kyle's bracelet. "I think we're growing close to something we shouldn't do tonight."

Kyle winces. "Yeah, sorry about that."

He turns the bracelet as he thinks about the other night with Renee. He knows he can't do the same thing with Aidan. As drawn as he is to the man, Kyle doesn't know him. They'll have coffee and maybe plan a scene. All Kyle has to do is be patient. He might want everything tonight, but it'll be better if he waits and does this the right way.

"Coffee on Sunday?" Aidan asks. "Or is that too soon?"

"Sunday's good," Kyle answers, glad he isn't the only one affected.

They move into safer topics like where they're meeting for coffee and how Aidan's enjoyed Enchanting Encounters so far and by the time Kyle's done with his cranberry juice he's settled if not completely satisfied.

"I need to head out," Kyle says. It's easier to walk away when he has Aidan's number in his phone and a coffee date planned for Sunday. "You know, people to jerk off to who aren't you."

Aidan laughs, surprised. "You're kind of a brat."

"Figured you should know that upfront. See you Sunday?"

It's a question in case Aidan's changed his mind, but Aidan isn't put off by his antics. He smiles again and says, "Sunday," before Kyle leaves.

WHEN HE ARRIVES at his apartment, Kyle pours himself a glass of water. He leans against his island counter and drinks it while he fumbles his jeans open with his other hand. Once he finishes his water, he puts his glass in the dishwasher and heads to his bedroom, fly open.

One of the benefits of living on his own is that he can wander around his apartment in whatever state of undress he wants.

He brushes his teeth because he knows once he's gotten off he'll be too tired to do it. He'll be lucky if he has enough energy to clean himself off before he's asleep.

He watches himself in the mirror as he brushes his teeth and takes in the spark in his eyes and his tousled hair and the way the small black triangle of his briefs peeks out from his open jeans. He pats his dick to remind it he hasn't forgotten tonight's most important plans then he rinses and spits.

Back in his bedroom, he strips his jeans off and tosses them in his *can be worn again* pile. His briefs go into his laundry basket. His T-shirt stays on so when he turns his face into his shoulder he can smell the faint scents of the club.

He grabs the lube off his bedside table and positions himself on his hands and knees on his bed. It reminds him of Richard's fingers around his hip and how good the spanking was. He turns the memory over in his head for a bit, need building inside him until he has to touch himself.

He fumbles to open the lube one-handed. This isn't his favorite position to jerk off in because it's hard to balance, but it's what he wants tonight. It's easier this way to imagine Richard's here and that he didn't stop spanking Kyle until he cried. It's easier to imagine the blows landing harder and harder until Kyle stopped begging to be spanked and begged to come instead.

Would Richard let him?

He would. Kyle begs real pretty when he wants something.

He wraps his hand around his cock and imagines it's Richard's instead. Would Richard be hesitant the first time he touched Kyle like this? Would his strokes be gentle, a counterpoint to the way his other hand presses hard against Kyle's skin? Would he slide his fingers into Kyle's mouth as he jerked him off or would he want to hear every noise Kyle makes, desperate and unfiltered?

Kyle digs his teeth into his bottom lip to keep from making those sounds now, and the fresh spark of pain makes his cock jerk in his grasp. He's embarrassingly close to coming, but he doesn't care. He was good tonight, and he deserves this.

His teeth press harder, and his thoughts flick to Aidan and his disapproval when Kyle bit his lip, and he drops his hand from his cock like it's burned him.

"Fuck," he pants because he was on the edge of coming before he pulled back. But Aidan told him he wasn't allowed to think about him when he got off, and even if Aidan won't know, Kyle agreed he wouldn't.

Besides, he doesn't need to. He has plenty of material to work with tonight. He closes his eyes and imagines Renee taking a more hands-on approach to mentorship.

Watch this time, she tells Richard. *Watch me take him apart and next time you can try.*

He imagines her nails scratching down his back, how his entire body would press into her touch, wanting everything she's giving and more. She wouldn't give him more, though. She always has a plan, and it doesn't matter how he bats his eyelashes or how filthy he is when he begs, she won't deviate. He likes the hard line she takes, appreciates how she sets limits and holds to them.

He strokes himself again, getting into the fantasy.

He drinks in the thought of Richard watching, of his entire focus on Kyle and the different ways to draw a reaction from him. With two people's attention on him, Kyle would show off, arching his back to put his ass on display, moaning every time Renee touches him in a way he likes. Renee would know he's showing off. Would she laugh at him? She has a way of laughing at him in scene—teasing, a little mean, but also fond—that brings him right to the edge every time.

Does Aidan know how to strike that balance?

"Shit."

Kyle flops onto his back, wincing as it wakes up the pain in his ass. His cock juts out between his legs, glistening with lube, and he's desperate to come. But despite all his resolve not to think about Aidan, he's thinking about Aidan.

"Fucking fuck," he groans.

He tentatively touches himself again, braced for the worst, but his thoughts drift to Renee again. She always gets so wet when she spanks him and sometimes when she's finished she'll grab a fistful of his hair and pull him between her legs to let him know she's done something nice for him and he should return the favor. Sometimes, she'll allow him to rub off against the bed while he eats her out. Other times, she makes him wait to jerk off until she's sprawled across the bed, sated and happy, and she'll watch as he strokes himself and tells her everything they did that he liked.

Would Aidan get off on spanking Kyle? Would he grind his cock between Kyle's sore cheeks afterward or jerk off on his sensitive skin?

Kyle drops his hands to his sides.

"Careful what you fucking wish for," he mutters before rolling off his bed.

He showers, the temperature cold enough to chase away his stubborn erection.

Chapter Six

THE FOLLOWING DAY, Kyle meets Richard for a Saturday afternoon coffee at Enchanting Encounters. Well, Richard has a coffee. Kyle's been awake long enough he doesn't need one. But anytime is a good time for a cinnamon roll, so he buys one with extra icing.

Richard looks the same as he did last night, tight T-shirt and well-fitting jeans, and Kyle's dick helpfully reminds him that he still hasn't come.

"I thought Renee would be here," Richard says after he finishes doctoring his coffee.

"We can reschedule if you want, but you two talked last night, and I figured you'd be more comfortable talking without her here. Some Doms get a little, uh, twitchy about having these kinds of talks in front of another Dom."

"Twitchy?"

Kyle shrugs. "Nicest word I could think of."

Richard's smile disappears just as easily as it had appeared. "Did I do a bunch of things wrong, then?"

"Hardly, but I didn't want you to feel uncomfortable. If you'd rather, we can talk about random stuff now and set up a meeting with Renee."

"I don't want *you* to be uncomfortable."

"You're sweet," Kyle says, and Richard flushes and looks down at his coffee. "But I've been doing this a while. I don't need Renee either."

"Neither do I."

Kyle leans back in his seat. "So, do you want to go first or do you want me to go first?"

"This goes both ways?"

"Always. Just because I've been at this longer than you doesn't mean I'm perfect. And who knows, we might scene together again, and if we do, then I want to make sure it's good for you."

"I don't think that'll be a problem," Richard says and his flush deepens.

Sweet, Kyle thinks again, but he doesn't say it out loud. "Why don't we start out easy? What'd you like?"

Richard looks around. There aren't very many people in the coffee shop—some couples enjoying an afternoon drink, a couple of people with books or on their cell phones. Kyle can tell the moment Richard remembers that they're still in the club because he relaxes and leans forward. There's no need to keep their voices down, there's no one here to offend or scandalize.

"I liked you," Richard says.

Kyle has a dozen responses to that, but he holds them back. Right now, it's important for Richard to become comfortable expressing his feelings. Flirting can come later.

"I liked how small you are."

"I'm not small, you're just a giant."

Richard grins, pleased. "I liked how easy you were to move around, I guess. Is that better?"

"I liked when you picked me up. That was hot. I liked it even better when you shoved my head down. There are a lot of subs into that kind of thing here. You'll be popular if it's a staple of your scenes. And you seem to like it."

"I do. I'm a big guy and I've always had to be careful, you know? Careful I didn't accidentally hurt someone even when I'm wrestling for the remote. But here I don't have to be careful. I mean, I do because I don't want to *hurt* hurt someone, but—" He flounders and looks to Kyle for help.

"You won't have trouble finding a partner who wants a few bruises after scening with you. And if you do want to...*hurt* hurt someone then there are people you can talk about that too."

Richard shakes his head. "I don't want to go that extreme."

"Entirely your choice." Kyle breaks off a piece of his cinnamon roll and eats it before he says, "Something else I liked was how you kept your free hand on me the whole time. I liked having the contact. It made me feel anchored to you."

"Renee told me you like to be touched."

"I do," Kyle says. It's a struggle to keep focused when his thoughts want to drift to imaging Richard and Renee talking about him while he wasn't there. He discreetly adjusts himself under the table. "I also liked how you talked out what you were going to do. When you said you were going to put me on the table, it gave me the chance to say no if I didn't want it."

Richard nods and curls his fingers around his coffee mug like he wishes he had a pencil. "Is this where we talk about what you didn't like?" he asks.

"There's nothing I didn't like. Sometimes your hand would catch me too low or your rhythm would stutter, but that takes practice. And it wasn't *bad*. You always brought me back to my headspace."

"You didn't go under, though."

"It doesn't happen every time, and it's not an indictment of you. Especially in demo scenes, I make an effort to stay clearheaded. It makes it harder for me to give you good feedback if I get lost in the scene. I still had a good time. Promise."

Richard flushes again, and Kyle wonders how red he could make Richard's face if he begged for all the things he wants Richard to do to him. That will have to wait, though. He's here for business.

"It was good enough you want to do something again?" Richard asks.

"Maybe. It's a good idea for you to scene with a couple other people so you can get an idea of what you like before we talk about a repeat. I can set you up with Lou if you want. He's a couple inches shorter than me, and size difference is apparently a thing for you."

"It's not a *thing*," Richard says. "But yeah, I like it."

"The whole point is doing things you like," Kyle reminds him. He eats some more of his cinnamon roll. "A few more things. Doing a scene with two Doms is always tricky. Renee and I know each other well enough that we didn't talk about as many things as we might have. As we probably should have." He flashes a smile. "See, always things to work on. I'm sure you noticed, but I was into the way she talked about me to you. Almost like she was cutting me out of the conversation."

Richard nods. "You liked it."

"A lot, and it's something she knows. But talking about someone instead of to someone, that's something to work out with your sub in advance. If they're not into it, then it can be jarring, like you're not treating them as a person."

"Did you feel that way?"

"No. I like it because I like being shown off. But it's something we should've talked about in advance. We made a point to go through what was okay for you and me before the scene, but we didn't do the same with me and Renee and that's our bad."

"It's okay," Richard says. He takes a sip of his coffee, looking thoughtful, so Kyle waits for him to work through whatever's going through his head. "I kind of liked it? Not in a—" he makes a jerk off motion with his hand "—kind of way but in a 'it would be nice to have a relationship like that someday' sort of way. I know it takes a long time to just know things about each other and to be able to read body language and stuff, but it would be nice."

Sweet and a romantic, Kyle thinks before the rest of it catches up to him. "Renee and I are casual." He can imagine her laughing her ass off if he told her that Richard thought they were relationship goals or whatever. "We know each other, but we're not—" He waves his hand around. "Uh, we're casual."

"So you're not with anyone?"

Depends on how tomorrow goes.

"I'm not in a formal relationship with anyone," Kyle answers. "I play with a bunch of people at Enchanting Encounters. So I can set you up with people I know or even nudge you toward people that might share your interests. On either side."

"It's a lot to think about," Richard says.

"Yeah, but you don't have to figure it all out today."

"I wish I could. I know what I want, but I still feel uncertain about a lot of things. I wish I was as confident as I want to be. You know?"

"Practice. It's how you build your confidence."

"Yeah." Richard looks as though he's been told that quite a few times. "I just wish I already had it."

"Practice isn't so bad. Was last night bad?"

"No, last night was really good."

"So, keep setting up scenes and keep having a good time. Before you know it, Doms will come to you as a mentor."

Richard looks terrified at the thought.

Kyle because he isn't always nice, laughs. "Maybe not that soon. But you're going to be fine."

"Yeah." Richard leans back in his chair. "So, we're done?"

"With the big scary talk, yeah. But you still have half a coffee and I have most of a cinnamon roll so let's talk about something less scary. What do you do for fun? Wait, let me grossly stereotype you first. You're tall and have a lot of muscles. How long did you play football for?"

Richard stares for a moment before he bursts out laughing. "Seriously?"

"Not football then? Basketball."

"I played basketball," Richard admits. He kicks Kyle under the table when he laughs at him. "I still do. A bunch of guys in my office are part of a rec league."

Kyle finishes his cinnamon roll while he listens to Richard talk about basketball, and he only makes one joke about Richard's ball handling skills. He's pretty proud of himself.

MEETING AIDAN FOR coffee is different than meeting Richard. For one, they don't meet at Enchanting Encounters. Kyle isn't in his territory, and it's strange. He has to remind himself three times that because they aren't meeting at the club they won't be able to scene right after coffee.

Aidan's already there when Kyle arrives and he checks his phone to make sure he's not late.

"You're good," Aidan tells him as they step into line. "I like to be early."

"Me too," Kyle says.

"I like to be first," Aidan amends.

He looks good today, in jeans and a light sweater in deference to the changing leaves. Kyle discreetly checks to see if the sweater has elbow pads.

"I'm not a complete fashion disaster," Aidan says with a smile.

Well, maybe not so discreetly. Kyle grins, unashamed of being caught out. "You rock the professor chic. Be honest, how many tweed blazers have you bought in the past month?"

"Bought?" Aidan shakes his head. "You never *buy* a tweed blazer. You have to find them at yard sales. They're more authentic that way."

Before Kyle can respond, a wave of people enter the shop, part of the morning rush, and Aidan looks around at the minimal seating and says, "I'll order while you hold down a table?"

"Sure. Regular coffee, medium."

"No pumpkin spice for you?"

"I like my coffee straight and boring." He can't resist his little smile or the way he brushes his hand against Aidan's. "Which, in case you're wondering, is the opposite of how I like my men."

The person behind them in line covers a laugh with their hand.

"Go," Aidan says, a smile tugging at his lips.

Kyle finds a two-person table tucked into the corner, as private as there is in here. It's still too close to the other tables for them to talk anything beyond surface likes and dislikes. This place is more suited to light-hearted flirting than anything serious. Kyle's a pro at flirting, but it's been two days since he's jerked off and he was hoping for permission and maybe some material to work with.

Two tables away from them, a younger mother tries to coax her stubborn toddler into eating pineapple. The boy keeps putting the pineapple in his mouth then spitting it out and looking at his mother, betrayed.

Kyle doesn't blame the kid. He doesn't like pineapple, especially when it's put in fruit cups. Its flavor has a way of seeping into everything and ruining it. He doesn't want his grapes or cantaloupe to taste like pineapple. He wants them to taste like themselves.

"That's quite the frown," Aidan says as he sets Kyle's drink in front of him and sits down.

"Ruminating on pineapple." He holds his hand out for Aidan's coffee. "Can I try it?"

"Sure, but you may not like it."

It smells sweet and tastes even sweeter, and Kyle wrinkles his nose as he hands it back. "What is that?"

"Chocolate caramel truffle." Aidan laughs, his eyes crinkling at the corners.

"Adventurous."

Aidan grins over the top of his coffee cup. "Which happens to be how I like my men."

Kyle laughs, loud and surprised. He's obsessed over Aidan for the past couple weeks, and he's thought plenty about how compatible they might be in bed, but he never let himself think about how compatible they'd be in other ways.

He *likes* Aidan.

Kyle settles into his seat and doesn't even pretend it's an accident when his feet nudge Aidan's under the table.

"So," Kyle says taking a sip of his boring coffee. "Art history."

"I don't remember mentioning that particular detail to you," Aidan says as his foot nudges Kyle's under the table.

Kyle's foot nudges back. It's their only point of contact. Kyle wants to place his hand on the table, an offering for another point of contact, but he's afraid it's too soon for that.

"I told you, you've been the talk of the club. Are you honestly going to tell me you haven't heard anything about me?"

"I've heard some things."

"They can't be too bad if you agreed to have coffee with me." He's fishing and isn't even being subtle. He finds subtle rarely gets him what he wants. It's always best to be direct.

Aidan glances around the coffee shop. The noise level's risen since they arrived, and the young mother and the little boy have been joined by another mother and her daughter. The little girl keeps swiping pieces of pineapple from the boy, and now he's decided he wants them because he starts crying.

"Maybe we can take a walk," Aidan suggests.

"Good thing you ordered our coffee to go."

He stands up, disappointed because it means there will be no footsie under the table. He's been looking forward to it since yesterday.

"I'm a planner," Aidan says, deadpan, and Kyle laughs before he leads them out of the café.

They're barely two steps from their table when it's taken over by two teenagers who look like there isn't enough coffee in the world to wake them up.

"I don't miss those days," Kyle says.

"I made it through grad school thanks to vats of coffee and the ability to power nap," Aidan says. "After that, I decided I was going to get my eight hours a night, no matter how boring it made me."

Aidan jumps ahead of him to hold the door, and Kyle's lips quirk in a smile. There's a bite in the air which makes Kyle tuck his free hand into his jacket pocket. He isn't bold enough to try to hold Aidan's hand yet, even if that would be a better way to keep warm. He takes a sip of his coffee and allows the heat of it to fight off the autumn chill.

"I've heard horror stories about grad school," Kyle says. "Every once in a while, if I'm stuck on a project, then I'll pull an all-nighter. Sometime between three and four a.m. when I'm hopped up on sugar and caffeine, I always manage a breakthrough. It's a completely useless breakthrough because I'm too scattered for anything else, but it unsticks me enough that after a long nap and real food I can actually get some work done."

"Project?" Aidan asks as he turns them down the sidewalk.

"I'm a graphic designer," Kyle answers, casual, like he isn't studying Aidan for his reaction. He hasn't had great experiences with traditional art people. There's a handful who think digital media corrupts the art world and another handful who think that because he uses a computer "anyone can do it."

Aidan raises his eyebrows at the scrutiny. "Is this where I cross myself and back away?"

"I dunno. Is digital media a sign that the end times are near?"

Aidan laughs. "You can't study the history of something unless it's in the past. There would be no art history without art future."

"Wow," Kyle drawls. "Deep."

"You're a brat."

He sounds fond, so Kyle's confident saying, "You like it."

"I do."

Feeling daring, Kyle asks, "Do you want to talk about what else you like?"

"In general, or about you?"

They turn into a little park and there are families down by the playground and a couple playing Frisbee with their dog, but there's also a path that leads away from all the activity. Aidan nudges Kyle down the path.

"Either." Kyle takes a sip of his coffee and notices that when they're standing side by side he has an inch or two on Aidan.

"I like how enthusiastic you are," Aidan says. He links his free arm through Kyle's as if they're out for a casual stroll and not discussing how their kinks line up.

Kyle drifts closer. "Sometimes I cross over from enthusiastic to pushy."

Normally, Kyle likes to talk himself up, but he doesn't want to do that here. He can scene with almost anyone at least once or twice, but he wants Aidan longer than that, which means he has to make sure some of his...bad habits aren't deal breakers. It's best to figure that out now before Kyle can get his hopes up even higher than they already are.

"Do you push looking for someone to push back?"

"Sometimes. Mostly, I just run my mouth and some people take it personally, like I'm disrespecting them or don't trust their plan."

It's put an end to more than one relationship Kyle was hoping to make long term, but he doesn't like feeling muzzled and his partners didn't like feeling undermined. Ultimately, they parted ways and they were both happier for it.

"That's what a safe word is for, you know?" Kyle continues because Aidan isn't pulling away. "Negotiations too. I don't sub for people I don't trust. I talk because that's who I am."

"I like my partners vocal," Aidan tells him, "and if I don't like what you're saying, then it's a challenge to make you talk about something else."

"You don't mind a challenge?"

"To a certain degree, no. There are certainly some instances where I want my sub to go down easy for me, but there are other times where I don't mind, and even enjoy, having to work for it."

That sounds like another point where they're compatible. Kyle takes a sip of his coffee before he asks the tough question. "What don't you like?"

"Student-teacher role play."

Kyle can't help his laugh. "Really?"

Aidan smiles back at him. "You have no idea how many people think I would be into it, but I find it incredibly uncomfortable."

"Fair enough. It's not something I've ever put much thought into, so no loss there."

"I struggle with sharing," Aidan adds.

Their steps slow but don't stop as Kyle turns this over. "Sharing like more than the two of us in a scene? Or sharing like using a public play space? Or sharing like exclusivity?"

"All three."

"I don't share with other subs," Kyle says, getting the easy one out of the way first. "I've done scenes with more than one Dom, but it's not something I need." He likes the extra attention, but he thinks with Aidan he'll have enough quality to make up for quantity. "I like public scenes, but they're not everyone's thing, and they're not something I need."

They walk a few steps in silence, both of them thinking, before Aidan says, "No thoughts on exclusivity?"

"I thought we were meeting for coffee and a casual chat," Kyle answers honestly. "This is beginning to sound like it might be more." And, as interested as Kyle is, he's not an impulsive person. Yeah, he's been thinking about Aidan for weeks, but he's only actually spoken to the man twice. "I'm not saying no," he says because Aidan pulls away a bit like he needs to distance himself before Kyle hurts him, "but I don't want to make any commitments until we've at least had a test run."

"A two-week trial period?" Aidan proposes. "Time for us to get to know each other better and have a few scenes so we can evaluate whether we're interested in something more."

They reach the end of the path. "Is two weeks long enough?"

"Depending on our schedules, we could fit in two or three in-person scenes and maybe something over the phone if that works for you."

"I don't mind the phone as long as it isn't too intense. I don't like to go too deep on my own because I don't deal well with long-distance aftercare."

"Would you be amenable to listening to me achieve orgasm over the phone?"

Amenable? Achieve orgasm? Kyle figures this is what happens when he falls for an academic.

"Yeah," Kyle says, "I'm *amenable* to that."

They turn to make their way back up the path.

"And the reverse?" Aidan asks. "If I talked you through your own release?"

"Pretty sure I figured that one out years ago," Kyle says with a grin. He knocks his shoulder against Aidan's before his smile slips into something more serious. "Tonight?"

"I thought I was moving too fast."

It's Kyle's turn to pull away slightly, heat rising in his cheeks. "You told me I couldn't come if I was thinking about you."

Aidan nods, but he doesn't look like he understands.

Kyle shrugs, and says, "So I haven't," as though it isn't a big deal.

Aidan's confusion gives way to something pleased, even a little smug, and he draws Kyle back against his side. "Are you telling me you've been thinking about me?"

Kyle's face is bright red now, and he mumbles, "Yes," and tries to turn away, but Aidan doesn't let him.

"Look at me," Aidan says.

Kyle looks at him.

"I like it. I like that you've been thinking about me. Maybe I'll call you tonight and you can tell me the kinds of things you've thought about."

"Please?" Kyle asks.

Aidan tosses his coffee into a nearby trash can so he can drag his thumb across Kyle's bottom lip. "You know how to be sweet when it suits you."

Kyle grins and doesn't deny it.

"So phone calls are good." Aidan's hand falls away from Kyle's mouth and he starts walking again.

Kyle can still feel the imprint of Aidan's finger against his skin. There's a faint buzz where it rested. Next time Aidan touches him like that he hopes they'll be somewhere more private so he can draw Aidan's thumb into his mouth.

"Phone calls are good but in-person will be better," Kyle says. He wants Aidan's hands on him and wants an opportunity to touch Aidan in return.

"Wednesday?" Aidan asks. "I have afternoon classes on Tuesdays and Thursdays so I can stay out later on Wednesday nights. If that's too soon, we can wait for the weekend."

"I can do Wednesday."

They're at the end of the side path, back to where it connects to the rest of the park. It feels like they've emerged from their own private woods, and Kyle figures this is as good a spot to let their conversation end as any. He has plenty to think about tonight, and even more to turn over in his head before Wednesday.

He needs to figure out a good first-time scene that hits enough of his favorites in case they don't scene again.

He said a two-week trial, Kyle reminds himself. *But that doesn't mean definite commitment. Even if he's interested now, there's no guarantee he'll continue to be.*

"Can I kiss you?" Aidan asks.

Kyle snaps out of his thoughts to see Aidan watching him, patient.

"Uh, now or in general?"

"Both, but specifically right now."

"Yeah," Kyle says, nodding. "You can kiss me."

Aidan smiles, a little quirk of his lips, before he leans in for a kiss, which doesn't last nearly as long as Kyle wishes it would.

When it's over, Aidan walks Kyle to his car.

A gentleman. How in the world did I manage to attract his attention?

Chapter Seven

ON MOST SUNDAY afternoons, Kyle hangs out with Jenny and Charlotte, but he doesn't visit them today. There's a giant smile permanently fixed to his face, and there's a bounce in his step, and he knows he wouldn't be able to hide either from them.

He doesn't want to hide his happiness, but he also isn't ready to talk about Aidan yet.

He can't help but feel like he's getting everything he wants, and he's lived too long to trust that feeling. He and Aidan have a two-week trial period to figure out if their interests line up enough to pursue something longer. If it turns out they're compatible, then he'll tell his friends.

For now, though, this is his thing, and he isn't willing to share.

After coffee, he considers an hour or two of work, but one glance at his computer tells him there's no way he'll be able to focus. It's more likely he'll end up surfing for porn, and he doesn't want to tease himself any further. He's on edge enough as it is.

He cleans his apartment instead.

He throws his clothes, his sheets, his towels, everything that can be washed into the washer then tackles his kitchen. He wipes down all the counters, uses the special stove cleaning solution to get rid of the grease splatter. He even cleans the front of his fridge and dusts off his toaster.

It's the most thorough clean he's given his apartment in a long time, but it keeps his mind occupied, and at the end of it, he's satisfied, if sweaty.

He tosses the clothes he used for cleaning into the basket for the next time he does laundry, then he showers.

Getting naked brings his thoughts back to Aidan, and he's half-hard by the time he's finished rinsing his hair. He doesn't usually do phone calls for a first scene, and it makes him nervous. He prefers in-person scenes, anyway because he likes to see his Dom. He feeds off their facial expressions and body language. And, even more than that, he enjoys being touched.

But he'll have to wait until he can have Aidan's hands on him. The idea of waiting, being *denied* makes heat curl in his belly. He has to leave the shower before he can follow that train of thought too far.

He eats dinner at his island counter and then he turns on HGTV. There's a show on about people looking for tiny houses to live in that Kyle gives a fraction of his attention. Mostly he stares at his phone where it rests on the arm of the couch. They didn't establish when Aidan would call. "Later this evening" is what they decided on because Kyle's into this kind of anticipation.

Kyle has low-grade secondhand claustrophobia once he's halfway through the episode. Watching people cram themselves into spaces too small for them makes him antsy, and he glances at his phone every few seconds as if he can wish Aidan into calling.

He sits through two episodes of the show before his phone rings. Even though he's been waiting for it, he still startles, and he checks the caller ID to make sure it's Aidan before he grins. He turns his TV off and waits for his phone to ring three times before he picks up because he doesn't want to appear too eager.

"Hey," Kyle answers, casual, as if he hasn't been looking forward to this for hours.

"Hey," Aidan says back, a mocking lilt to the word. "How was the rest of your afternoon?"

"Good," he answers. *I compulsively cleaned my entire apartment even though you're not even coming over.* "Relaxed, showered, watched some TV."

"Did you eat?"

"I did. Do you want to know what?" Kyle's careful here to make sure he doesn't come across as sarcastic or bratty. Aidan's doing the right thing, making sure Kyle's ready for their scene, and Kyle won't dismiss his effort.

"Not unless you want to tell me."

"Not particularly."

Kyle can hear Aidan's smile as he says, "I had chicken pot pie—one of the ones you stick in your freezer and then pop in the microwave when you're hungry."

He winces on behalf of Aidan's stomach and stretches out across his couch. "I thought you were a professor and not a student."

"Is that judgement I hear?" Aidan asks, amused.

"I'm not judging the pot pie, just the quality. They're not hard to make."

Kyle would offer to cook for Aidan, but that's a pretty big step seeing as they're on their first scene of a trial period. It's the kind of step to take once they've progressed out of scenes at the clubs and to one of their places. Kyle still itches to make the offer.

"I'll keep that in mind," Aidan says. "Is there anything else you need to take care of tonight?"

Kyle glances down at his lap. "Besides the obvious?"

"That's something I'm intending to take care of."

And there's that switch in his voice. It's deeper now, the traces of easygoing humor gone. Kyle doesn't try to hide his groan. If Aidan isn't here to see what he does to Kyle, then Kyle wants to make sure he can hear.

"We didn't talk specifics earlier," Aidan says, perfectly composed. "I would like to do that now."

"Okay."

Kyle debates slipping a hand into his pants. There's a thin line between negotiation and foreplay for him, and given how long he's been without release, there's no way he won't grow hard listening to Aidan talk. Unless Aidan starts saying things like *achieve orgasm* again.

"Don't touch yourself," Aidan tells him.

Kyle sighs. He didn't think he'd get away with it, but it was worth a try.

"Where are your hands?"

"One is holding my phone to my ear and the other is tucked under my head."

"Good. Keep them there unless it grows uncomfortable."

Kyle wiggles a little before he says, "I can do that."

"Earlier we discussed you talking me through your fantasies about me," Aidan says. "Are you still amenable to that?"

Fuck. Kyle's dick twitches in his pants. Is this the start of *linguistic boners?*

"Yeah."

Aidan clears his throat.

"Yes," Kyle corrects. "I'm good with that."

"What are your thoughts on orgasm delay and denial?"

"I like it, but it's what I've been doing since Friday night, so I'd like to come tonight. If you want to make me wait for it, then I will."

"And if I want to make you work for it?"

Kyle's fist closes around empty air. He wishes it was on his cock so he could do something about the rush of heat he feels. "I'm cool with that too." There's a telltale waver in his voice.

"Would you like to conduct this scene on your couch or your bed?"

"Bed." Kyle sits up. "It's where I've done all my thinking about you."

There's a moment of silence on the other line, and Kyle congratulates himself on affecting Aidan at least a fraction of the amount Aidan's affected him. Aidan's all big words and steady voice, and Kyle appreciates the control, but he also wants to shatter it.

"I want you to prepare your room for our scene and the immediate aftermath, starting with a glass of water or juice from your fridge. Put it on your nightstand once you have it."

"Is this really necessary?" Kyle asks, even as he heads into his kitchen. This isn't his first scene. He knows how to take care of himself afterward when his Dom either can't linger or isn't in the same place as him.

"Yes."

Kyle fetches himself a glass of water and sets it on his nightstand along with a bowl of hot water and a washcloth. He brushes his teeth while on speakerphone then picks out his favorite pajamas and pulls them on.

He does it all with Aidan's voice in his ear, telling him he's done well or instructing him what to do next.

"Huh," Kyle says when he climbs onto his bed—comforter stripped back—and realizes he's still half-hard. "I didn't think I'd be into that."

"Following orders?"

"Mundane ones."

Kyle frowns, unsure whether to be pleased he's still learning things about himself or annoyed because he's apparently been keeping secrets from himself. Normally, he doesn't enjoy being micromanaged, and he prefers his in-scene orders to be more...fun, and this is unexpected.

"There's nothing mundane about making sure you're taken care of. I would prefer to be the one doing all this, but since I can't, you make an adequate replacement."

"Adequate?" Kyle squawks. "I think you're selling me a little short."

"Maybe," Aidan says, and Kyle can hear his smile over the phone.

Kyle stretches out on his bed, head resting on his pillow, feet reaching toward his comforter, bunched at the end of his bed to minimize clean-up. Everything's taken care of except for him, but that isn't his responsibility. It's Aidan's.

Kyle hums, a happy little sound, and lets his legs splay open.

"You didn't pick up your phone on the first ring," Aidan says. "How long did you wait before you picked up?"

Here we go, Kyle thinks. Then, *am I already in trouble?*

"Three," Kyle says. "Or two, depending on how you count."

"How would you count?"

"Three. I knew it was you calling before I looked at the Caller ID, but I waited because I didn't want to seem overeager."

"You made me wait," Aidan says, "and now I'm going to make you wait. Three rings so three times you'll get close to coming, and three times I'll pull you back."

Kyle twists his free hand in his T-shirt so he doesn't touch himself and closes his eyes.

"Are you still okay with tonight's plan?" Aidan asks.

"Yeah." Kyle clears his throat. "Definitely, yeah."

"Place your phone on your nightstand," Aidan tells him. "I want both of your hands free for this."

Kyle sets it on the nightstand then settles back on his bed. "Can you still hear me okay?"

"I can. Are you ready to begin?"

Anticipation prickles down his spine. "I'm ready."

"Push the waistband of your pajama pants down. I don't want you leaking on the front of your pants because you're wearing these to bed."

Kyle lifts his hips and tugs the waistband down enough to free his cock. When he settles back on his bed, the sheets are cool against his bare ass.

"I could take my pants completely off," Kyle says.

"There's not much point. It's not like I'm there to see you."

"Shit," Kyle mutters, squirming on his bed. A bead of precome wells up at the tip of his cock which means he pulled his pants down just in time. "Can I touch myself? Please?"

"Yes, but dominant hand only."

Kyle wraps his left hand around his cock and hisses a slow breath out through his teeth. He's touched himself like this thousands of times in his life, but it feels particularly good right now. The last few times he's touched himself he immediately had to stop because he wasn't allowed to think about Aidan, but now he can.

He can think about Aidan in his own bedroom, listening to Kyle's breathing, heavy and growing heavier. He can imagine Aidan in the room with him or Aidan's hand wrapped around him.

"How is it?" Aidan asks. "Too dry?"

"I like it a little dry, but I'm thinking I'll be at this for a while so lube would be good."

"You can put some on your hand," Aidan says. There's no change in his tone, nothing to suggest this is doing anything for him, and Kyle frowns as he reaches into his nightstand for his lube. He wanted the phone scene so they could do something, and because patience isn't one of his strengths, but he misses the connection of being in the same room.

Using only his left hand means he can't rub his hands together to warm the lube up, and he wrinkles his nose when he wraps his hand around his cock again. It doesn't take long to warm-up though, and he falls into a familiar rhythm as he strokes himself.

"You wanted your clothes off earlier," Aidan says.

Kyle closes his eyes so he can pretend Aidan's here. He slows his strokes while Aidan's voice washes over him.

"You want to show off for me even though I'm not there," Aidan continues.

"I thought it would make it easier for you to imagine what I look like."

Aidan laughs, a low warm chuckle. "Have you forgotten that I've already seen you naked? I don't need any help in the visualization department."

Kyle rubs his thumb over the tip of his cock, precome joining the mess of the lube. "Did you like what you saw?"

"I couldn't see much more than your ass," Aidan says and Kyle groans and strokes himself faster. Aidan laughs again. "You like that? What if it was my first night in the club, and I'd never seen you before? That the first time I saw you all I saw was a pink ass, raised high in the air, *begging* to be hit harder?"

"I like that a lot." His breath comes quicker now, and the sound of his hand on his cock is loud to his ears. He hopes Aidan can hear it through the phone, hopes Aidan knows how much he's affected Kyle with only a few phrases. "Would you hit me harder?"

"If you were on that table for anyone to use, yes."

There's something about Aidan's delivery, how casual he is, that makes Kyle whimper. What if that was how Friday night played out?

What if Kyle was an offering for anyone passing through? And Aidan saw him and laid his hands on him? Would Kyle have begged him to stay? Would Aidan spoil him for everyone else? Would Kyle even know it was him?

Kyle's abs tighten and his balls draw up, and he barely rips his hand off his cock before he comes. "Fuck," he gasps. "I—I'm not touching myself anymore."

"Too close?" Aidan asks.

"Yes."

"I'm glad you obeyed my instructions." Aidan's words soothe most of Kyle's displeasure at being denied. "I want you to pick up the dry hand towel and wipe your hand off."

Kyle's thorough as he wipes the lube from his hand, cleaning each finger and between them, taking his time until his breathing is steadier.

"I haven't seen *you* naked," Kyle says. His throat is dry, so he takes a sip of water.

"You haven't."

"Is it too late to ask to make this a video call?"

"Yes, but it wouldn't matter, anyway. I'm completely clothed. Does that ruin your fantasy?"

"A little bit, yeah."

"I'm wearing argyle socks."

Kyle laughs, unable to help it. "Is this where I say you'd look better if you took them off?"

"This is where you tell me if you're ready to touch yourself again."

Kyle glances down his body. He's still hard, but he doesn't feel as if he'll fly apart the second he touches himself. One denial, two more to go. *That* he isn't sure he's ready for.

One at a time. Let Aidan guide you through it.

"Yeah," Kyle says only a faint tremor in his voice. "I'm ready."

"Non-dominant hand this time."

It's odd to use his right hand. He isn't used to it, and he doesn't grip tight enough and then too tight, but his dick doesn't care because, right now, any kind of contact is good contact.

"Tell me what you look like," Aidan says.

"Clothed." Kyle can't quite keep all the bitterness out of his voice.

"Does that make it harder to put on a show for yourself?"

"It takes effort to look the way I do. There's nothing wrong with appreciating it."

"There isn't. Maybe next time I'll appreciate all your work, but for right now I want you to tell me what you look like."

Kyle looks down at himself again. "Uh, I'm hard."

Aidan laughs. "I figured."

"Um." Kyle licks his lips and takes a deep breath as he studies his appearance. "I'm in a white T-shirt. It's a sleep shirt because it's wearing through in places. I can see my skin through some of the faded patches."

"Good," Aidan praises. "Keep going."

It's easier now that he knows what Aidan's looking for, and he doesn't feel as silly with Aidan encouraging him. "The fabric's bunched over my stomach. It trembles every time I clench my abs. My pants are shoved down just a couple inches like I couldn't be bothered to take them off all the way before I touched myself."

It's not completely true—his pants are like this because Aidan told him to do it, but it's still a hot visual. He tightens his grip as he imagines what it would look like if Aidan hadn't let do even this much? What if he had to draw himself out through the slit in his pants? He'd be completely clothed, put together except for the obscene jut of his cock, flushed and red and protruding from his pants.

He groans and his hand stutters in its rhythm.

"Tell me what you're thinking," Aidan commands. "I want to know what made you have that reaction."

"I'm imagining if you told me I couldn't even pull my pants down. These are sleep pants, so they have the flap in the front. Thought about you making me get off like that instead."

"What if we did it the other way around?" Aidan asks. "What if the first time I let you put your mouth on me, I only unzipped enough to pull my cock out?"

Kyle would be completely naked because in his fantasies he never wears clothes, and it would put him in direct contrast to Aidan. Aidan would be in a button-down with a sweater over it and his stupid khakis and argyle socks, and he'd probably even have shoes on, as if showing Kyle the outline of his toes would be too scandalous.

"You're a tease," Kyle accuses. Fantasy Aidan all covered up is a tease and real-life Aidan might even be worse because he's far away, leaving Kyle to make do with his imagination.

"I'd give you what you want. I'd fuck your mouth until all you could do was choke on my cock. My guess is that's the only way to shut you up.

You'd rest there on your knees and let me use you, and when I came, I'd do it all over your face and your chest. And then I'd push you down until you were on your back, let you sprawl out on the floor, covered in my come, while you jerked yourself off."

That hits so many of Kyle's buttons he has to drop his hand from his cock to his thigh and dig his fingers into his skin, the sharp burst of pain unpleasant enough to pull him back from the edge.

"Can we—" Kyle has to pause to take a few deep breaths. "Can we put that on the list of things we do together?"

"All of it? Or the part where we spend an afternoon where you wear nothing but my come?"

Kyle makes a low, pained sound as his dick throbs, needing release and not getting it.

"Too much?" Aidan asks.

"Unless you're about to let me come."

"I'm not. Wipe your hands off."

"I'll need more lube after this."

"You have my permission to use as much as you need."

"Okay."

There's a beat of silence before Aidan says, "Thank me for giving you permission."

Kyle shifts on his bed and wishes he was on his stomach so he could turn his face into his pillow. Aidan isn't even here, but Kyle can almost feel the weight of his gaze through the phone.

"Thank you," Kyle mumbles.

"Good or bad?" Aidan asks.

"Good."

Good in a bad kind of way, the kind which twists him all up with embarrassment and leaves him blushing but also harder than he was before. It's the kind of good he doesn't like to admit to but that a skilled Dom usually picks up on.

"You can be sweet, you only need some nudging."

Kyle turns even redder. This isn't helping him bring himself back under control. "By the way, if I start having khaki boners them I'm blaming you."

"You really hate my pants."

"I'd rather see you in nothing," Kyle says, words accompanied by a sleazy grin even though Aidan isn't here to see it.

"I suppose I walked into that one. You've kept yourself from coming twice. Are you good to do it again?"

"I'm not keeping myself. *You* told me not to." If Kyle had his way, then he would've come by now.

"I'm not there, which means you're choosing to do what I asked. I wish I was there, though. I bet you look beautiful when you listen to me."

Kyle's skin feels too tight, as if he'll burst if he doesn't touch himself, if he doesn't find a way to hold himself together. "Can I touch myself? Please?"

"Yes. Don't forget, you wanted more lube."

"Will you be this fussy when we're doing a scene together in person?" Kyle asks as he squeezes more lube onto his hand.

"I think you like being micromanaged."

Kyle's conspicuously quiet. He does enjoy being micromanaged, more than he realized, and more than he wants to admit. He likes orgasm delay and denial, even enjoyed cock cages the few times he experimented with them because he likes giving his control to someone else. He likes the idea that he can't be trusted to make choices for himself.

He's never explored it to the extent he thinks Aidan might want to, but he's willing to try.

"Do you want me to do it right now?" Aidan asks.

"Yes," Kyle whispers, voice almost too quiet to carry through the phone.

Aidan takes pity on him because he doesn't make Kyle ask again. "Grip yourself in one hand and angle your cock up toward yourself."

Kyle obeys with a shaky hand. "I've done it."

"Good. Now, with your other hand, use the tip of your pointer finger to circle your slit."

Kyle bites his lip as he does it, a few muffled sounds escaping. He's so sensitive this feels like torture. He squeezes his eyes shut and a few tears slip out. His body trembles, on the edge of something he knows he can't have. He whimpers and wishes Aidan was here to see him. Wishes Aidan was here to brush the tears away and tell him how good he's been.

"Work outward in a spiral until you've touched the whole head of your cock. Have you ever done this before?"

"I haven't."

It feels good but too good, the kind that verges on painful.

"Do you like it?"

"Yes."

"Thank me," Aidan tells him. "Thank me for teaching you something new about pleasuring yourself."

Aidan's words are like a bolt of pure arousal, and Kyle gasps and has to drop his hands to the bed. His body curls in on itself like he's trying to come but doesn't have enough push for it. His breath hitches on the next inhale, and he doesn't quite pull in enough air. It makes him gasp for his next breath and his chest burns, needing more air than he can breathe in.

He's coming undone, and he can't do anything to stop it.

"Stay with me," Aidan commands, his voice calling Kyle back to himself.

"I'm here." Kyle takes a few steadying breaths. "You're really fucking good at this. At me."

"I want this to be enjoyable for you."

"It is." Kyle wipes the fresh tears from his eyes and remembers what Aidan told him to do before he was overwhelmed. "Um, thank you." He clears his throat. "Thank you for teaching me something new."

"You're welcome."

"Fuck." Kyle's fingers twitch, desperate to be wrapped around his dick. "Can I come now? You said three times I couldn't, and it's been three. Please, I need this."

"Soon," Aidan promises. He doesn't sound as steady as he did before, as if Kyle's managed to affect him a fraction of how Aidan's affected him. "It's my turn first. Put your hands above your head, out of reach of temptation."

Kyle wraps his hands around the slats in his headboard, designed expressly for this purpose. He looks up at his ceiling because it's safer than looking down at himself.

"Can I talk to you while you get yourself off?" Kyle asks. He can't see Aidan and he can't touch him, but he can give him his voice.

"I would like that. You mentioned how you've spent a lot of time thinking about me when you were trying to jerk off. Will you tell me about that?"

"Of course. Uh, when I got back from the club the other night, my ass tender from my spanking, I wondered if you'd get hard from hitting me. I bet you would. I'd beg for your touch and then thank you when I got it."

Kyle can hear Aidan breathing hard through the phone. He flexes his fingers around the slats in his headboard. "I thought about you spanking my ass red and then jerking off on me like it wasn't enough to mark me with your hands. You needed to mark me up more, needed to put a claim on me so no one in the audience thought they had a right to me when you were done."

Aidan's so quiet when he comes, Kyle can barely pick it up over the phone, and it makes him feel cheated. It makes him even more eager for Wednesday night. He'll make sure to negotiate to have Aidan's hands on him and to be able to see the man come. Listening through the phone makes him greedy, makes him want to see every reaction Aidan has.

But more immediately he wants to come. He squeezes the slats of his headboard and twists his hips, chasing something he's not sure he can have.

"You can touch yourself," Aidan tells him.

Kyle groans when he wraps his hand around his length. He thrusts into the tight grip of his fist and tips his head back to show off the expanse of his throat even though Aidan isn't here to wrap a hand around Kyle's neck or even bite into the thin skin there. Now that Kyle's brought it up, he wants Aidan's marks.

He wants Aidan's hands on him, gentle enough to feel good and then rough enough to leave behind reminders of tonight.

"Does it feel good?" Aidan asks.

Is he fucking serious? It's been days *since I've come and tonight has been torture.*

Kyle keeps his thoughts to himself. He doesn't want to be denied again because he can't keep his mouth in check. He lets Aidan hear his noises instead; little breathy moans, the hitches in his breath when he twists his wrist just right, the panted *ahs* as he gets close.

"Can I?" Kyle asks. "Please? I've been good, right? Patient? Please, I—"

"You can come," Aidan tells him, "but you have to thank me for the privilege."

"Thank you," Kyle says as he strokes himself faster, almost frantic. "Thank you for letting me listen to you. Thank you for permission—ah— for me to come."

"You're welcome."

Kyle's orgasm knocks him breathless, his entire bodying tightening up then going boneless, the most relaxed he's been in days. Collapsed against his pillow, he glances down his body, at his pajama pants and rumpled white T-shirt, and he thinks if he didn't have a palm full of come, then he could fall asleep like this.

"Wipe your hands on the hand towel," Aidan tells him, his voice softer, but no less certain than before. "Tell me when they're mostly clean."

Kyle's too wrung out to even want to move that much, but it's easier to clean himself up when Aidan's prompting too. Honestly, and he isn't proud of this, if he was alone, he'd probably wipe his hand on his pants or maybe his shirt, pull up his pants, and call it a night.

Instead, his wipes his hands on the towel and says, "Clean."

"Now the washcloth. Is it still warm?"

Kyle lifts the washcloth from the bowl and wrings most of the water out so it won't drip. "Still warm."

"Good. Clean your hands then gently wash the rest of you."

Kyle does as he's told. "All done."

"Pull your pajama pants up and drink your water."

Kyle pulls the waistband of his pajamas pants up. He's fully clothed now and cleaned up, no signs that he was up to anything this evening except for the pleasant warmth which has spread through his whole body. He wants to wrap himself up in his blanket and tuck all of Aidan's praise tonight around him and fall asleep, but he can't yet.

Aidan told him to do something.

Kyle pushes into a sitting position and takes the water off his nightstand.

"Once you're finished I want you to pull your blankets up over you."

Kyle doesn't rush his water, but he doesn't dawdle either, excited to be under his blankets. His comforter is heavy enough that it almost feels like someone's holding him once he's situated. It would be better if Aidan was here, though.

"You're a cuddler?" Aidan asks.

Kyle winces and hopes he didn't say too much of that out loud. "Yeah." He moves his phone from the nightstand to his pillow so Aidan's as close as he can be. "It helps ground me after a scene."

"Are you okay on your own right now?"

"Yeah." Kyle wiggles a hand free to cover a yawn. "Will you talk to me for a bit?"

"Of course. I can talk to you until you fall asleep if you'd like."

"Yeah. What're you teaching about tomorrow?"

"My first class is on the role of art in religion. We're studying Hinduism right now, and tomorrow's lecture focuses on stonework. I'm sure it'll spark a discussion over what does and doesn't qualify as art. Despite being an advanced class, many of my students still think art is limited to what can be framed."

Kyle drifts off to the sound of Aidan's voice.

Chapter Eight

KYLE WAKES UP in stages, stretching his legs out toward the foot of his bed then reaching his arms up until his knuckles knock against the wall. Finally, he opens his eyes and smiles as the light filters in through his curtains.

"Good morning to me," he says.

He showers, still smiling about last night, and takes care of everything he was too tired to do after his scene with Aidan. His shirt and his pajama pants are dropped in his laundry basket, the now cold water is dumped in the sink, and the bowl and the empty glass are put in the dishwasher.

He keeps his good mood as he makes breakfast—eggs, toast, and tater tots—and he's only a little surprised when his phone dings halfway through shoveling food in his mouth.

Aidan: *How are you feeling this morning?*

Kyle: *Good. You?*

Aidan: *Nothing sore? Head in a good place?*

Kyle rolls his eyes at his phone because Aidan isn't here to see it. He appreciates the concern, and maybe it's even a little sweet, but Kyle can handle himself. He's met Doms who assume because he likes to sub it means he's fragile. That's bullshit is what it is, and he doesn't think Aidan's trying to coddle him, but he doesn't like feeling hovered over.

Kyle: *Everything's good. You didn't answer.*

Aidan: *I am quite well this morning. You'll let me know if anything changes?*

Kyle: *Yes. When does your first class start?*

Aidan: *Five minutes. My students are all here except the one who is late every class. A product of poor scheduling. He only has ten minutes to cross the entire campus, and it's a fifteen-minute walk if you have a brisk pace.*

Kyle takes a picture of his breakfast and sends it with his next message.

Kyle: *Bet my breakfast was better than yours.*

Aidan: *Does coffee count as breakfast? I'm turning my phone off for class, but I'll turn it back on in an hour. Will you be okay?*

Kyle: *Yes. I'm going to eat breakfast, do some work, and probably drag Jenny over for lunch. I'll send you pictures of that too.*

Kyle doesn't get a response to his last text, but he doesn't expect one until later. He finishes breakfast and settles down in front of his laptop, ready to work. He's clear-headed and focused the way he gets after a good scene. There's no itch under his skin and he's able to sit for an entire hour before he has to stand up and walk around.

He sinks even deeper into his project afterward, and he loses track of him. He's just putting the finishing touches on his first draft of a mailing for a local energy company when there's a knock at his door.

"Did you forget about me?" Jenny asks, barging in. She pauses in the doorway, surprised to see him sitting at his computer. "Someone's motivated today."

"I'm feeling good."

"Uh-huh," Jenny says. She nudges the door shut with her foot and fixes him with a look that demands answers. "Any reason?"

Kyle flushes bright red and holds a finger up for quiet so he can email Brett Panik with the draft of the mailing. That done, he checks his email to make sure there's nothing urgent that requires his attention. Unfortunately, there isn't, which means it's time to face Jenny.

"Lunch?" he asks, hoping to distract her.

"Lunch and a story." She hops onto his kitchen counter. "What were you up to last night?"

"I spent the night in." It's the truth, even if it's not the *truth,* and Kyle feels a flicker of guilt which he quickly extinguishes.

Things with Aidan are still new, and this is a trial period which means it's not even official. If they agree to a longer term together, he'll tell his friends. He doesn't want to get their hopes up over nothing. And he doesn't want to invite a thousand questions until he knows Aidan better.

"Huh," Jenny says. "When you didn't text me about lunch, I figured you had someone over."

Kyle shuts his computer and investigates the contents of his fridge. "So you thought you'd investigate? What if I still had someone over?"

"You never let people stay past breakfast so I knew it was safe."

Sadly, it's true. When Kyle does invite people to his apartment they usually scene that night and, if they stay, he makes breakfast for them before he sends his partner on their way. Making breakfast is polite, but asking them to stay later is inviting them into his life. It's not something he's had a lot of opportunity to do.

He thinks he could work with Aidan in his apartment. Maybe Aidan could grade papers or plan lessons while Kyle worked on his projects. Probably not right away, Aidan is still too distracting, but maybe once they've spent more time together.

And he's getting ahead of himself again.

"Pasta?" Kyle asks.

"You have the stuff for the sauce?"

"The cream sauce or the one with bite to it?"

"Cream. I don't like my food fighting back."

Kyle laughs. "Yeah, I can do the cream sauce. I think I even have a fresh tomato. I can dice that up, maybe even make some chicken, and we can have a proper lunch."

"I don't know what I'd do without you to feed me. Probably waste away."

Kyle grabs a few things out of the fridge and then sets the oven to preheat before debating what kind of pasta to use. Penne? Rigatoni? Spaghetti?

"It's more fun cooking for two than for one," Kyle says.

He learned to cook when he was a kid since his mom worked full-time, and his dad had never been interested in the kitchen. They ate out a lot because it was easier, and his mom was usually too tired after work to cook. It was the source of one of the many fights his parents had.

His mom didn't make his school lunches either, and after a couple years of buying cafeteria food he didn't even like, he would add a few things to the grocery list every week and make his own lunches.

His parents eventually divorced. Then his mom remarried and Kyle had two brothers and a sister and new dad, and he didn't know what to make of them. He mostly stuck to his policy of taking care of himself and staying under the radar.

By this point, he had grown beyond peanut butter and jelly slapped on two slices of bread and he'd make himself turkey sandwiches with tomato and guacamole. He even packed homemade desserts instead of cookies bought at the store.

His stepdad was the first person he ever cooked for when the man asked if Kyle could make lunch for him too in the mornings. Kyle had spent months braced for the "I'm not your dad but I want to be" talk, and he'd been caught off-guard by the request. Then pleased.

Cooking was something he cared about, something he was good at, but something no one had ever noticed before.

It was Brian, his stepdad, who gave him his first cookbook, and Kyle grew more adventurous with the things he made. They eventually had the "I'd like to be your dad" conversation while sautéing mushrooms with all the windows in the kitchen open because Kyle's mom loved mushrooms on her steak but hated the way the smell would linger in the kitchen.

Cooking with Brian led to dinners with the whole family sitting down together, the grown-ups talking about work while the kids complained about school, and it was different than Kyle and his mom and his dad when they'd eat somewhere with TVs mounted on the walls so they didn't have to talk.

Kyle gave his family a reason to sit down together, and he thinks that's what he loves about cooking, how he can use it to draw people he cares about closer to him. And because food is better when it tastes good.

Kyle grabs the penne from the pantry. "How's Charlotte?"

"She's working more, which I guess is good, but it means she's gone longer."

"The library was able to keep its funding then?"

Kyle sets a pot of water to boil and digs the chicken out of the fridge. Penne with a creamy Alfredo sauce, chicken, fresh tomato, and fresh parmesan will make for a damn good lunch. He wants to text Aidan a picture of the final product, but he doesn't want Jenny to ask more questions.

"The town approved the budget, and she received the grant she applied for, so she's starting a toddler reading program. It's for little kids and a parent or babysitter or whoever, and they'll read some books as a group and then sing songs and do a craft. She's really excited about it."

"That sounds adorable. Maybe I'll borrow someone's baby for a morning and show up to let her know I support her. Who do we know with babies?"

Jenny laughs. "Or you could use your library card and check out a couple books. Probably better than stealing someone's baby."

"I said borrow. And who has the time to read books? I have to support myself. *And* you, apparently." He shakes a third of the penne into the pot then eyes Jenny and adds some more.

"And yet you still have time in your busy schedule to woo mysterious men. I heard your scene with Richard was quite the hit."

Kyle waggles his eyebrows. "My ass certainly thought so."

Jenny groans. "If you weren't making me food, I would walk out on you right now."

Kyle grins and dumps the rest of the penne into the pot. There's nothing wrong with having leftovers.

KYLE THROWS HIMSELF into his work because it's a good distraction from Wednesday night. He doesn't want to build his anticipation up to the point where whatever happens will be a disappointment. He texts with Aidan on and off, but it's more Aidan checking in and Kyle sending back pictures of whatever he's eating.

It's one of the stranger relationships he's had with a scene partner, but he kind of likes it.

Wednesday night, they meet at the club's café at seven, and Kyle orders an orange juice and a chocolate-frosted brownie.

"Want some?" Kyle offers when he catches Aidan staring.

Aidan quickly shakes his head. "It's an odd combination."

"As long as I drink the juice first, it's fine." Kyle flashes a smile and takes a long sip of his juice. When he's done, he flicks his tongue over his bottom lip to taste the lingering sweetness of the juice and grins when he catches Aidan staring. "So, is this a double? Are we talking about Sunday and planning tonight?"

"I'd like to, if you're okay with it."

Aidan's in khakis again which Kyle hopes is a joke and not some indication of the limits of his wardrobe. Kyle knows when Lou is in a committed relationship he enjoys when his Dom picks his clothes out for him, but Kyle's not sure he could do that with Aidan. Kyle has a reputation to uphold and that means no cuffed khakis.

"Sunday night was good," Kyle says. "You have a nice voice so doing it over the phone wasn't bad, but I still would've preferred to see you."

Aidan smiles and drops his gaze to the table like he's shy or maybe even embarrassed, which is at odds with Kyle's memories of the other night. Aidan is so smooth, so confident in scene, but out of it, he's more reserved than Kyle would expect.

Aidan picks up Kyle's napkin and tears it into small pieces before he says, "I pushed you more than I should have. We didn't talk about humiliation before the scene. It was something I picked up on, but I should've waited to try it until we had talked about it."

It takes Kyle a couple of seconds to realize Aidan's apologizing for being able to read Kyle so well he could do it over the phone.

"I liked it," Kyle says. When Aidan doesn't look up, he reaches across the table to touch his wrist and gain his attention. "I have stoplights for a reason, if I didn't like it, I could've told you. And, if I needed to, then I could've hung up."

"It's still bad etiquette."

"It's okay. We're still getting to know each other. We'll stumble across each other's likes and dislikes. But we can be more specific with this scene, if it makes you feel better."

"It does."

Kyle takes another sip of his juice. "What did you have in mind for tonight?"

"Something basic. You're leaving a club or a bar after not having found anyone that catches your eye."

"Mm, and then you swoop in to rescue me from a lonely night?"

Aidan flushes again. "I know it's an overused scene, but I wanted something simple for our first time."

"Classics are classics for a reason. Besides, I like early scenes to be ones I've done before. It makes it easier to compare them."

"But no pressure."

Kyle's still resting his hand on Aidan's wrist, so he squeezes it briefly before he lets go. "I'm sure it'll be good."

Aidan looks more confident as he sits up in his chair. "What do you want from tonight?"

Kyle wants a lot of things. But he voices the one that's topping his list. "Is it too soon to ask if you'll fuck me?"

"Condoms."

"Of course." Maybe if they agree to an extension after their trial period, then they can look into going without but definitely not for their first time. "You can rough me up a bit. Bruises and scratches anywhere clothes will hide are fine. Light verbal humiliation is good." Kyle flashes Aidan a smile. "How specific are we talking?"

"How would you like me to fuck you?" Aidan asks.

Kyle knows they're in the club, but the bluntness still catches him off-guard and he says, "Uh," and reaches down to adjust himself in his pants.

The expression on Aidan's face is too sharp to be a smile. "Up against the wall since I'm finding you outside a bar?"

Kyle imagines stumbling out of Enchanting Encounters, disappointed with the night, and seeing Aidan who offers Kyle everything he'd been looking for. But what exactly is it he wants? "The wall is good. Did I mention you can push me around?"

Aidan's expression edges into something closer to a smirk. "You did. So, I find you outside the bar after you've struck out and I give you exactly what you want?"

"Hey. After I struck out? If I showed interest in someone, then I wouldn't be going home alone."

Aidan laughs. "Fine. There's no one in the bar who catches your eye and you leave disappointed and discouraged. Is that better?"

"Perfect. I'm waiting for a cab when you show up and my night takes a turn for the better. Do you want titles for this?"

Aidan shakes his head. "Not since we're pretending we're strangers. If you use titles, I want you using them for *me*."

Kyle has to remind himself he's at a little two-person table in the café and is *not* allowed to jerk off, no matter how much he might want to. "I'll use stoplights if I need them. Does that cover everything?"

"I think we're good," Aidan says. "Do you want your brownie?"

Kyle finishes his juice and tosses it in a nearby trash can. "Nah, I'll put it in the aftercare room. I'm going to book us something to use tonight and get ready. Give me fifteen minutes? I'll tell Lis to expect you, and she'll direct you to the right room."

"Fifteen minutes?" Aidan asks and he sounds disappointed, as if it's longer than he wants to wait.

Kyle grins, glad he's not the only one who's been looking forward to this. "Fifteen minutes and then I'm yours for the rest of the night."

He leaves before he gives into temptation and kisses Aidan in the café. They'll never make it to their room if they start things here, and Kyle's excited for tonight's plans. A little more patience, and he'll have everything he wants.

He winds his way through the club, waves to a few people, but he shakes his head whenever anyone tries to stop him for a chat.

"You have plans tonight?" Lou asks, surprised, when he manages to catch Kyle.

"What can I say?" Kyle asks. "I'm popular."

He laughs and dances away from Lou's groan. Lis is the concierge on duty, and Kyle offers her his most charming smile.

Lis rolls her eyes. "Someone has something fun planned tonight. What do you need?"

"An alley/suite combination if you have one."

"Classic," Lis says. She taps a few buttons on her computer. "We have a couple of those open. Room Five work for you?"

"Thanks. When Aidan comes through will you let him know?"

Lis stops typing. "Aidan?" She smiles. "I heard you were interested in him. Congrats."

"Just a scene," Kyle says.

"If he doesn't want another one after tonight, then there's something wrong with him."

"This is why you have my heart," Kyle tells her. He kisses her cheek. "Everyone else only gets my body."

"Okay, Romeo." She laughs and hands him a signature pad. "Sign. There's lube and condoms in both rooms. Do you need anything else?"

"Can you up the temperature a few degrees? I don't like being cold."

"And we know more clothes isn't an option."

"You know me so well." Kyle checks his phone. "I need fifteen minutes to get ready. If Aidan shows up early will you stall him?"

"Of course." She hands him a key to the room.

"Seriously," Kyle tells her as he walks backwards in the direction of the room. "My heart, it's yours." He blows her a kiss, and she laughs as she shoos him along.

Room Five opens into a narrow hallway. The walls are dark red and painted to look like bricks, realistic enough that Kyle runs his fingers over the paint to make sure it's not actually brick. The wall is smooth, something Kyle will be thankful for later when he's pressed up against it.

The lighting in the room is dim, the lights covered in shades to make them look like streetlights, two framing the door Kyle came through and two framing the only other door in the room.

Kyle opens that door and the dim alleyway leads into a standard hotel room—big bed and small en suite bathroom. There are grander rooms than this, but those are for different scenes. Kyle's been in those too: rooms with ornate beds; with a study desk which can withstand the weight of two people; a bathroom designed for sex.

This isn't like those. This is an aftercare room, designed for post-scene care. Kyle inspects the mini-fridge to make sure it's stocked and he sets his brownie down next to a row of water bottles.

He gives the room one last look to make sure it has everything he needs before he enters the alleyway again. He gives his eyes a couple of moments to adjust to the change in lighting then he hunts for the lube. There's a trashcan at the end of the short hallway that's actually a trashcan, but there's what looks like a mailbox fixed to the wall above it.

The flag is up and Kyle grins as he thinks *you've got mail* and opens the box to find more lube packets and condoms than they could possibly need for the night.

He glances at his phone, and he only has a few minutes left which means he has to make this quick. He glances at the door to the hallway, anticipation bubbling in his stomach as he thinks about Aidan walking through the door to find him with his pants around his knees, prepping himself out in the open.

Maybe a different time. That isn't what this scene is, which means he has to hurry up or he won't be ready when Aidan arrives.

Chapter Nine

KYLE LEANS AGAINST the wall near the bedroom door when music filters through the room's speakers. Well, it's not music so much as background noise: muffled shouting, foreign cursing, cars beeping, and cab drivers yelling. There's even the faint pounding of a bass as if Kyle's actually outside a club and not in a room of make-believe.

The music is Lis's way of warning Kyle that Aidan's on his way. Kyle loosens his posture as he leans against the wall.

It doesn't take long before he hears the click of the lock, loud even over the rest of the noise in the room. He turns his head to the door to see if whoever's there is worth his attention.

Aidan—the stranger—comes through the door with his head ducked and his hands in his pockets like he hadn't found anyone worth his time in there either. He takes the opportunity to study the man while he's distracted. He's in dark wash jeans and a long-sleeve thermal, the buttons undone and still not showing off enough skin.

Kyle quickly glances down at his phone before the stranger can catch him staring.

"Hey," the stranger says.

Kyle looks up from his phone enough to say, "Hey," back but then he lowers his gaze again.

"It's a little early to head out," the guy says.

His voice is closer, and when Kyle glances up again, the guy's only a foot away. He's close enough to touch if he wanted to.

Kyle shrugs, aiming for bored. "Nothing caught my eye. I figured it's best to cut my losses. Besides, I know I'm a sure thing." He smirks a little and makes the universal sign for jerking off.

"Crude." The stranger hooks a finger through one of Kyle's belt loops, bringing them even closer. There's only a few inches between them now, and Kyle breathes embarrassingly fast given there's no actual contact between them. But there's a promise of more in how close they are, in the way the guy stares, demanding Kyle give his attention to him.

Kyle was going to finish tonight at home where he was guaranteed to have a good time, but this guy is the most interesting person he's seen all night. Because he's slouching, Kyle has to glance up at him, and he doesn't bother to hide the way he evaluates him like he's determining whether further conversation is a waste of both their time.

"I'd hate to see you leave without getting what you want," the stranger says.

It's such a *line* that Kyle can't help his scoff. "Let me guess, you want to fuck all my disappointment away?" Kyle rolls his eyes.

"I didn't say anything about fucking, but if that's what you want, then I can accommodate."

He steps forward until their hips are lined up, and Kyle can feel the hard press of the man's dick against his thigh.

Kyle instinctually rolls his hips against the stranger's, chasing what's being offered. He throws him a lazy smile and says, "I think I'll be the one accommodating, if you know what I mean."

He's kissed in a response, the stranger cupping Kyle's chin in one hand and holding him still as their lips touch. It's a slow, coaxing kiss as if the stranger's trying to draw a reaction from Kyle, and when he pulls back, Kyle tries to follow, but the hand on his chin holds him where he is.

Kyle's head thunks back against the wall. "Is there more of that?" he asks. He drags his tongue across his bottom lip as if he can keep the taste of the stranger in his mouth.

"I guess that depends." The man glances down at the phone still clutched in Kyle's hand. "Have you already called a cab?"

"If I have?"

"Then we better make this quick. Unless you're up for an audience."

Kyle's gasp would be noticeable even if the stranger wasn't still holding his jaw. The corner of the man's lips pull up in a smirk, and Kyle wishes his back wasn't against the wall so he had somewhere to hide.

"Is that how it is?" the man asks.

He flushes but doesn't say anything, and the man looks over his shoulder at the door leading to the club Kyle's given up on.

"Maybe you weren't looking for a quick grind on the dance floor tonight. Maybe you were looking for a guy who'd take you out back where anyone might see you."

"Oh, fuck," Kyle says. His hips push up against the stranger's, searching for any kind of friction he can get. If the stranger would slot a thigh between his, then Kyle could probably come like this, with an unfamiliar voice in his ear and unfamiliar hands on his body.

"So," the stranger says. "Do you have a cab on the way?"

Kyle shakes his head.

"Do you want me to call you one?"

This is Kyle's chance to duck out if this wasn't what he wanted out of the night. He's glad the man's giving him the opportunity to leave, but he doesn't plan on taking him up on it.

"I'm good."

The stranger grins and plucks the phone out of Kyle's hands and slips it into his own back pocket. "Then I guess it's just us. I'm Aidan, by the way."

"Kyle."

The stranger—Aidan—drops his hand from Kyle's chin and presses light kisses against the imprints his fingers left behind. "What do you want, Kyle?" he asks.

Kyle's dick shouldn't jump because of the way someone says his name, but it definitely does. "I get to pick?"

"You're the one who had big plans for the night." Both of Aidan's hands are on Kyle's hips now, and his thumbs sneak under the material of his T-shirt to rub across Kyle's skin. "Besides, I'll only give you what you ask for." Aidan leans in to whisper the last few words against Kyle's ear.

Kyle whimpers and tries to chase the press of Aidan's body, but Aidan holds him against the wall and steps away so Kyle's hips roll against empty air.

"What do you want?" Aidan asks again, and Kyle wants so many things he's not sure where to begin.

But one thing stands out more than the rest and Kyle says, "Fuck me." He's not quite pleading, but he's close. If Aidan keeps teasing him like this, then it won't be long before Kyle begs. "Please, I want you to fuck me."

Aidan *laughs,* a sharp, amused sound that hits Kyle right in the gut, and he's not sure whether to turn away from Aidan or jut his chin out and demand what's so funny. His cock doesn't have any conflicted feelings; it strains against Kyle's zipper, and if Kyle doesn't take his pants off soon, then he's afraid he'll have a zipper imprint on his dick.

Something else for Aidan to laugh about.

Kyle's face is bright red now. When he told Aidan they were good for light humiliation, he didn't realize they were *this* good. He risks a glance at Aidan's face and wonders what he'll say next. Something soothing? Or will he twist Kyle up even more? Kyle isn't sure which one he wants.

This is why you have a Dom, so you don't have to make these decisions. He's in Aidan's hands, literally and figuratively.

"That's all you want?" Aidan asks. He slides his hands up Kyle's stomach until his palms press hot against Kyle's nipples. "No foreplay, no sweet kisses? Just a good, hard fuck against the wall?"

Kyle squirms, trying to get some friction, but Aidan laughs again and pulls his hands back. Kyle doesn't dare move from the wall.

"I told you, I'd only give you what you asked for," Aidan tells him. "It's not my fault you have such a one-track mind. Turn around."

There's no room for Kyle to argue, nothing for him to do but obey. He does glare a little as he turns around, and when he braces himself against the wall, he doesn't push his ass out, doesn't put on a show, his own form of petty revenge.

Aidan just laughs at him again, the sound low and curling around Kyle's dick like a physical touch.

He steps closer and rests his hands on the button of Kyle's jeans. "Did you change your mind? You don't want it anymore?"

Kyle holds out until he realizes Aidan will loom behind him, hands on Kyle's pants until he says it. Another wave of heat rushes to his face. He doesn't know how his body has blood to spare between his face and his cock. Maybe that's why it takes so long for him to find the words he needs.

"Fuck me," he says, more snarl than anything else. "Like you said you would."

Aidan leans in until his front is a long line of heat against Kyle's back. "Like you asked me to," he counters. Then he pops the button on Kyle's jeans and drags the zipper down. Aidan hooks his fingers in Kyle's briefs next, and he drags both them and his jeans down to just above his knees.

Kyle tries to kick them lower, but Aidan shoves him against the wall with surprising, stunning force.

"You stay where I put you," Aidan tells him, and Kyle shudders all the way down to his toes.

"Please." Kyle shimmies like he can lose his pants this way. "It'll be better for you if I have more room to move."

"Better for me, huh? Or maybe you're just desperate to spread your legs. Desperate enough to put on a full show for anyone who happens to pass by. No, we'll try for at least a little modesty."

Kyle forgot they were outside the club and that anyone could come out here and see them. Not that they'd get much of a view if they did. With Aidan behind him, Kyle's almost entirely blocked from view. Will this mean Aidan won't strip down? Kyle's disappointed, even though he can't see Aidan.

Aidan backs off enough so Kyle can lean against the wall, rather than be pinned against it. Then he nudges Kyle's ankles apart with his foot.

"Hmm, maybe you're right," Aidan says before he pushes Kyle's jeans down another inch. "Have to make sure you can spread your legs enough for me to get in there."

"Fuck," Kyle says and he presses his cheek against the cool wall.

"I know, one-track mind." Aidan grabs two handfuls of Kyle's ass and squeezes. He dips his fingers in Kyle's crack. "Huh." His fingers trace the trail of lube to Kyle's hole, but all he does is rest his thumb there. He doesn't press in, no matter how much Kyle wiggles and tries to encourage him.

Aidan grabs a fistful of Kyle's hair with his free hand and turns Kyle's head so they're looking at each other. "You weren't going home to jerk off. You were going home to shove something in this greedy ass of yours." He dips his thumb in, just the tip, to prove his point.

Kyle groans and pushes his hips back into the touch, but Aidan pulls away, leaving him empty and aching.

"I wanted to make sure I was ready," Kyle says even though he doesn't need to defend himself.

"Are you?" Aidan pulls Kyle's ass cheeks apart like he's *inspecting* him, and Kyle's running so hot he thinks he might explode. "Show me how you got yourself ready. First, hold yourself open."

Kyle sucks in desperate breaths as he does what he was told, his hands replacing Aidan's. Aidan steps away, and Kyle can't hold back his whine because this is the opposite of what he wants, but a moment later, he feels something drip on his ass.

Lube.

Aidan's squeezing a packet of lube on his ass, careless, almost dismissive, and Kyle says, "Thank you," before he realizes the words are in his head.

Aidan's quiet for a moment, and Kyle squeezes his eyes shut as his heart hammers away and he wonders if this is when everything becomes too much. But then Aidan runs a hand through Kyle's hair, affectionate. "What a polite boy," he says and Kyle whimpers, but Aidan's touch is enough to hold Kyle together. "Now, put your fingers in your ass."

Kyle shoves two fingers in without much finesse because he needs to touch himself. He needs a hand on his cock more than he needs fingers in his ass, but this is what he's allowed to have, so he'll make the most of it.

"Did you do this at home?" Aidan asks, conversational. "A warm-up before going out?"

Kyle nods.

"The lube was too fresh for that to be the only time," Aidan continues. He's standing almost on top of Kyle, close enough for Kyle's wrist to drag against Aidan's jeans every time he moves his hand. "Did you do it again in the club? Did you slip into the bathroom for a quick finger bang? Did you have to bite your other wrist to keep from moaning?"

Kyle moans now, and he jabs his fingers into himself, and it hurts, but he can't concentrate enough to do it right. He can't think, can't *move* with Aidan this close, saying all this in his ear. Is this really the same guy who walked arm-in-arm with him at the park and apologized for being too aggressive in their last scene?

Aidan tsks and knocks Kyle's hand away from his ass. "You're not doing a very good job. If that's how you did it earlier, then it's no wonder you're not satisfied. Do you want me to help you?"

There's lube dripping down Kyle's ass because he couldn't even manage to push most of it in, let alone stretch himself, and he nods, face red with shame and frustration and arousal.

Aidan tsks again, the sound going straight to Kyle's dick. "Words."

"Please," Kyle says. He rests his forehead against the wall and squeezes his eyes shut like that makes it easier.

"What's the rule?" Aidan asks.

Kyle has to ask for what he wants. *Fuck.* He squirms as he builds up the courage to say, "Please finger me."

"Why?" Aidan presses gentle kisses against the back of Kyle's neck like they're having sweet, first time in a bed sex. As if Kyle isn't shoved up against a wall with his pants around his knees.

"Because your dick'll hurt going in if you don't," Kyle snaps.

Aidan laughs. "Try again."

Kyle hangs his head. "Because I can't do it right myself."

Aidan pats Kyle's hip. "That wasn't so hard, was it?"

Aidan gathers up the lube with two fingers and presses it into Kyle, stretching him the way Kyle hadn't managed to do earlier. It feels good, almost too good, and Kyle cants his hips back, wanting more. He's already on the edge, face hot, heart pounding, dick fucking hard, and this is both too much and not nearly enough.

"Three, please?" Kyle asks. He's being good, following the rules, making sure he asks for what he wants.

"This quickly? Are you sure you're ready?"

"Yes." Kyle wants to be filled, with Aidan's fingers or his cock, wants to be fucked until he can't think. Until all he can do is pant and beg for more.

"Hmm," Aidan says as he pushes his fingers in deeper like he's testing to see if Kyle's ready. His thumb rubs around Kyle's rim, making Kyle groan and clench around him. Aidan is a fucking tease. How didn't he notice this before? "I think I'll wait a bit longer."

Kyle knocks his head against the wall.

"None of that now," Aidan chides. He grabs a fistful of Kyle's hair and holds him tight. "I'm the only one who's allowed to hurt you. Besides, you like being teased. Your toy at home couldn't give this to you. It must've felt like your lucky night when you saw me come out of the club."

Yes, but this guy clearly doesn't need his ego stroked. He's full of himself enough as it is. "It'd be a better night if you held up your end of our deal."

Aidan works a third finger in. "Is this what you wanted?"

"I want your dick," Kyle grits out. He strains against the hand in his hair just to feel a spark of pain. He wants more. He wants Aidan tugging on his hair while he fucks him or maybe gripping his hips hard enough to bruise. He wants to be held and fucked and overwhelmed and he wants it *now*.

"Yes," Aidan says and he pulls all three fingers out of Kyle, which is the opposite of what he needs. "You've been very insistent on that."

"Hope it's worth it," Kyle snarks, hoping Aidan will shove his face into the wall. Instead, Aidan ruffles Kyle's hair before he pulls that hand back too.

"I guess you'll find out."

Kyle looks down at his dick, still standing tall. Could he get away with touching himself? Aidan never said he couldn't. He hasn't mentioned Kyle's dick at all, come to think of it. Will he have to ask permission for this too? Kyle flushes hotter.

Then he sucks in a breath because he feels the nudge of something thicker and blunter than fingers at his hole. *Fucking finally.*

"Is this what you want?" Aidan asks.

"Yes."

"You can do better than that."

"You *promised*," Kyle whines and maybe it's stupid to dig his heels in here when he's so close to what he craves, but he has to have some pride.

"Tell me."

Okay, maybe pride isn't something he cares all that much about because he caves quickly. "Please," he whispers, shame and arousal coiling tight in his gut. "Please, put your dick in me. I want to feel it. I want you to fuck me."

"Better," Aidan says. He drags his cock through Kyle's crack, the head catching on Kyle's rim. "Louder, now. I thought you wanted someone to hear and come investigate. Maybe they'll be as desperate for cock as you are. Maybe they'll want nothing more than to get their mouth on your cock while I fuck you."

Honestly, Kyle doesn't care about anyone else at this point. He just wants Aidan filling him up. "Please, fuck me. I've been thinking about this all night. I fingered myself hoping I'd find someone like you. Someone who'd push me up against the wall and make me take it." All true, Kyle *has* been thinking about this. "Please, it'll feel so good. I, ah—"

Aidan shoves in all at once, knocking the words out of Kyle's mouth.

For about two seconds anyway. "Thank you," Kyle says, voice climbing as Aidan digs his fingers into his hips so he can hold Kyle in place as he fucks into him. "This is exactly what I wanted. Your cock feels so good inside of me. Ah—" Kyle braces his hands on the wall and shoves back so he can get Aidan even deeper.

"That's it," Aidan tells him. "Are you getting exactly what you wanted?"

"Yes," Kyle hisses. His cock is dripping precome on the floor.

"Is this what you were hoping for when you fingered yourself earlier?"

Kyle had shoved his pants down just like this while he waited for Aidan to get to the room, and he thought about what the scene would be like when he got himself ready. He thought about how good Aidan's cock would feel in him, how it would reach deeper than Kyle's fingers, how it would stretch him more than Kyle was going to stretch himself.

That's exactly what he's getting. But Kyle hadn't put enough thought into what Aidan would *say*. He hadn't realized how easily Aidan would break him down, how easily he'd twist Kyle up into a panting, begging *mess*.

"Better," he manages to say between punishing thrusts. "This is better."

"Good." There's genuine pleasure in Aidan's voice.

It's a little out of character, and they both realize it at the same time because Aidan begins to fuck into him harder as if to make up for the moment of gentleness.

"I hope you can come like this," Aidan says, cock driving up into Kyle, making him go up on his toes every time.

It's not a question, but it's kind of a question, and Kyle takes stock of himself. His cock feels like it's been ready to burst for *hours* and while he can't always come without a hand on him, he thinks he'll be able to do it tonight.

"Yeah," Kyle says. "I can."

"Good," Aidan tells him. "Because all you asked for was to get fucked, so I'm not putting a hand on you. Though maybe you planned it that way. Did you want to show off for me? Is that why you set it up like this?"

It isn't—Kyle didn't realize at the time that what he asked for was going to be the only thing he got—but he can't say he's disappointed. Because he *does* want to show off. He wants Aidan to be impressed with him. Wants Aidan to like him.

Aidan crowds closer and his hips slow to a dirty grind, his cock never leaving Kyle's ass. "Are you going to show off for me?"

"Yes."

A soft kiss to the back of his neck, right against his hairline where Kyle first starts to sweat. "What do you need?"

"Fuck me," Kyle tells him. "Hard. Like before."

He braces his hands on the wall so he's ready for it when Aidan starts pounding into him again. The impact of the thrusts goes from the tips of his fingers all the way down to his toes. He's practically vibrating with each snap of Aidan's hips. His cock is hard and swinging between his legs, and he lets his pleasure build. Every thrust of Aidan's cock, every press of his fingertips into Kyle's skin, every grunt and groan in Kyle's ear pushes him closer and closer.

He pushes past too much, past the almost overwhelming need to get a hand on himself so it will all be over. He pushes himself until he's trembling on the edge of something that seems too big, like he can't.

But he can.

"Please," he says, and his voice sounds wrecked, doesn't even sound like him. "I can come, I'm ready. Please, let me, tell me I can. I want to be good for you. Let me be good for you. *Please.*"

"Come," Aidan says, and as if Kyle's body is hardwired to Aidan's voice, he comes.

He pounds his fists into the wall as his cock pulses and empties. Coming like this, without a hand on him, always leaves him wiped afterwards, like he needs that hand on his cock to hold himself together.

"Amazing," Aidan tells him.

Kyle shivers with the praise.

"You can finish," he says. They didn't talk about that, whether Kyle's okay with being fucked after he's come. The answer is yes.

"I don't think that'll going to be a problem," Aidan says.

It takes Kyle's muddied brain a couple seconds to figure that out. "You?" he asks, and he can't help but feel cheated. Not only did he not get to see any of Aidan, he didn't get to fully experience Aidan coming inside him.

"Me," Aidan answers. He moves his hands from gripping Kyle's hips and wraps them around Kyle's waist, tight enough to hold him up but loose enough that Kyle can still breathe with ease.

The edge has slipped out of Aidan's voice, and it's like a signal to Kyle's brain, *scene over.* He's never met anyone who can flip their switch like that.

"I'm about to pull out," Aidan warns him.

Even with the warning, it's still uncomfortable. Kyle hates the minute or two after sex when he feels *empty.* The sounds of Aidan disposing of the condom are distinct, but Kyle stays leaning against the wall. It's comfier than he'd expect.

"So," Aidan says, returning. He rubs his hand over the skin of Kyle's hip, where there are sure to be bruises later. "Are you still disappointed?"

Kyle can't help his laugh. He tries to turn around so he can see Aidan, but he gets caught up in his jeans and ends up almost falling on his face instead.

"Easy now," Aidan says. "Are you ready to go into the other room? We can clean you up."

"Yeah."

Kyle hikes his pants up high enough to walk which mostly seems like a waste of energy because as soon as they're in the other room, he drops them back down again. He grabs a wet wipe from the bedside table because he doesn't want to wait for a washcloth, and he cleans himself up.

By the time Aidan emerges from the bathroom, Kyle has his briefs on, and he's under the covers.

"Didn't want to wait?" Aidan asks.

"No," Kyle answers, hoping that's not a problem. Aidan had been…fussy over the phone, but Kyle figured that was because he was struggling with how to do long-distance aftercare. It's entirely possible that that's just how he is.

Aidan stands in the bathroom doorway, wiping his hands. "Okay," he says. His tone doesn't give Kyle an idea of whether or not he's made the right choice. And this is his real struggle with new Doms. He's fine in scene, he has no problem reading body language or tone there, and he knows how to make up for mistakes he's made. It's different once the scene's over. It leaves him off-balance.

He wants to burrow under his blanket, but he sits up instead. Whoever designed this room gave it a padded headboard, so Kyle doesn't have to figure out how to prop pillows up behind him. He silently thanks the designer, whoever they are.

"I still have my brownie," Kyle says. "We can split it."

Aidan considers him from the doorway, staring long enough that Kyle starts to get a little antsy.

"Okay," Aidan finally says. "You should drink something too." He leaves the bathroom in favor of the mini-fridge. "I'm guessing you know what they carry here."

"Water," Kyle says. He doesn't want to drink all of it at once which means juice is out unless he wants to put off eating his brownie. Which he doesn't. He got a good scene, a good fucking, and now he wants to round his night out the right way.

Aidan's mysteriously in plaid sleep pants and a T-shirt, a detail that doesn't click until he's sitting next to Kyle in the bed.

"You brought a change of clothes?" Kyle asks.

To his surprise, Aidan *blushes*. "Yes," he answers, the word way too simple for his reaction.

"There's more to it than that," Kyle says.

Aidan breaks off a piece of brownie and holds it out. Kyle could take it with his fingers, but he dips his head down instead, draws the bite into his mouth with his tongue.

"I brought an overnight bag." Aidan hands Kyle a bottle of water. "On the phone, you said you liked to cuddle."

So Aidan packed sleep clothes and, if Kyle's reading him right, clothes for work tomorrow in case Kyle wanted to stay here all night. If this wasn't their first in-person scene, if they knew each other better and Kyle knew their boundaries, he'd lean in kiss Aidan right now. He's not sure if that's a thing they do. He presses himself closer to Aidan's side and takes a sip of his water.

"I do," he finally answers. "But I also have a flexible work schedule. I can stay here the whole night without causing any problems."

"So can I," Aidan says. "I have everything I need for class in my car, and I have clothes in my bag for teaching in. If you want to stay the night, then we can."

"What about what you want?" This street goes both ways.

Something unpleasant flashes through Aidan's eyes, too quick for Kyle to figure out what exactly it is.

"I want to try this brownie of yours," Aidan says, which isn't the answer Kyle was looking for, but he lets it go. If Aidan doesn't mind staying the night, then Kyle won't talk him out of it.

Chapter Ten

AN UNFAMILIAR ALARM pulls Kyle out of his pleasant dreams, and he groans as his very nice human pillow moves because it means his head falls onto the pillow. But the pillow is also comfortable, so Kyle wraps his arms around it and says, "Five more minutes," which is his standard response to any alarm.

"You can have five more minutes," Aidan tells him, and he cards his hand through Kyle's hair which both threatens to send Kyle back to the land of dreams and makes him put more effort into being awake because he doesn't want to miss any of this.

He's fallen asleep in plenty of beds at Enchanting Encounters, but he doesn't often wake up with someone else next to him. This is nice—not just the scalp massage, which Kyle shamelessly pushes into, but also just having someone here with him.

"You can even have an hour if you want," Aidan says, "but I need to leave for work soon."

"Shower?" Kyle asks. He could drag himself out of bed to shower with Aidan. It isn't lost on him that never mind seeing Aidan completely naked, he still hasn't even seen him with his shirt off.

"Sleep," Aidan says. He presses a kiss to Kyle's forehead and climbs out of bed.

Kyle's too stunned to move right away, and by the time he pushes up on his elbows, the bathroom door is already closed and maybe even locked. He sighs and turns onto his back so he can stare up at the ceiling.

If they were at Kyle's apartment, then he'd make breakfast for Aidan before he left. As it is, Aidan will probably stop at a drive-thru on his way to work, and it's not bad, but Kyle could do better.

You're moving too fast. This is a trial period. It's still too soon to know where this is headed.

The problem is he knows exactly where he wants this to go. He wants shared breakfast in the morning and soft kisses before work and, yeah, he's moving way too fast.

His forehead tingles with the imprint of Aidan's lips.

He flips back onto his stomach so he can scream into his pillow.

KYLE ENJOYS TAKING care of people. It's an instinct he's had since he was a kid, and it's grown stronger as he's gotten older.

Sometimes, he takes care of people by going to his knees for them.

Sometimes, he likes to do it by cooking for them.

When he arrives home after a solo shower at the club, he's antsy and restless in a way he usually isn't after a good scene. After two hours of administrative work, because he can't handle anything creative right now, he gives up on being productive and bakes.

The baking itself is good because it's a familiar process, and all he has to do is follow a set of instructions, but his favorite part of baking and cooking is when he presents what he's made to someone else.

Maybe it's because he wasn't able to make Aidan breakfast this morning or maybe it's something else, but Kyle feels better once he has a Tupperware in his hands and a destination in mind.

It's a short walk to the library, and it's a beautiful day for a stroll, and maybe a bit of light exercise is exactly what he needs so he can focus this afternoon.

He waves to the woman at the front desk and lets himself into the break room where the rest of the small staff is eating lunch.

Charlotte's in the far corner, a book open in front of her as she pops grapes into her mouth. She's only twenty-four, but she dresses like she's decades older. In the last year, she's seen the light when it comes to leggings because she spends so much time crouching down or sitting on the floor with little kids, but she insists on pairing them with cardigans or vests she dug out of her grandmother's attic.

Today, Charlotte's sporting gray leggings and a black vest with the whole Peanuts cast on the back. At least it's better than the palm tree dress she wears for *Chicka Chicka Boom Boom* readings.

Kyle knocks on the open break room door and says, "Special delivery."

"New books?" one of the librarians asks, turning around. She looks disappointed when she sees it's only Kyle. "Not books."

Kyle holds up his Tupperware. "I brought cookies, though."

The promise of cookies draws Charlotte away from her book, and she looks surprised but then smiles when she sees Kyle. "What brings you here?"

Kyle shakes his Tupperware. "I thought I'd spread some good cheer."

"It's September...?"

"And that means you don't want cookies? It's all good. I'm sure I can find some other haggard public employees who want some pumpkin chocolate chip cookies."

"Did you say pumpkin?" Mrs. Melrose, the oldest of the librarians, calls from the circulation desk. "Save two of those for me!"

"Will do," Kyle promises.

When he turns back to Charlotte, she's eyeing him as though she can draw his secrets out with the power of her stare. Past evidence has made him pretty sure she's a mind reader, so he doesn't bother to say anything. He just sets the cookies on the table and takes the empty seat next to her.

He places his computer bag on the floor and ignores it even though he brought it with him so he could pretend he's here to be productive and not simply to hand out cookies in an effort to make himself feel better.

Charlotte slips her bookmark into her book so she can close it then she takes her glasses off and lets them hang down like a strange kind of necklace. Because Charlotte's fully embraced the librarian lifestyle and wears her glasses on a *chain*.

Kyle pops the top off his Tupperware and sets two cookies aside for Mrs. Melrose before he takes one for himself.

"What brings you out here?" Charlotte asks.

"Atmosphere. I have a lot of work to do, and I need somewhere I can concentrate. Libraries seem like the kind of place that cultivate creative energy."

"Uh-huh," Charlotte says. "So does Panera."

One of her coworkers squawks her protest, and Charlotte hands her a cookie before taking one for herself.

"It's too noisy," Kyle says. On some days, he needs the steady buzz of background noise, but today even the sound of his own breathing is enough to distract him. "I thought I'd try and tap into the quiet energy here."

"And you just happened to have cookies to bring?"

"I didn't want to show up empty-handed."

"The whole point of the library is that it's free. You didn't need to bring anything. Did you at least eat lunch before you came over?"

"Of course." He never bakes on an empty stomach because that's a road that leads to sugar highs and crashes. "Enjoy your cookies. I'm off to work for a bit."

"You'll want to find a table upstairs. We're doing Kids' Corner down here in half an hour."

He takes his bag upstairs to the adult floor which is two big rooms connected by a smaller room with the circulation desk at one end and the staircase at the other. The room on the left is the Young Adult section, and it's full of couches and a couple of tables for study groups. To the right, where Kyle goes, is not only shelf after shelf of books, but there's a whole section of carrel desks.

There are ones tucked up against bookshelves and ones against the walls. At least half have a window view, but he knows he'll only be distracted if he chooses one of them. He sits at a desk that faces shelves of encyclopedias and pulls out his computer.

It takes him a bit to find his rhythm, but he does find it, sinking deep enough into his project that he's startled by the knock on his carrel.

He glances over to see Charlotte standing there. "Hey," she says.

Kyle turns his laptop toward her. "Which looks better, the one on the left or the right?"

Charlotte puts her glasses on. "Am I supposed to see a difference?"

"The backgrounds are different shades of blue."

Charlotte squints. "Really?"

"Yeah. Guess that means it doesn't matter which one I go with."

"Come on," Charlotte tells him, "I'll walk you to your car."

"You go on ahead, I want to finish this first." Maybe if he changes the font? Or repositions the picture. He changes the font type then the font color and frowns because neither of those look any better. "Besides, I walked here."

"You walked?" Charlotte repeats. "It's thirty minutes on a good day."

"I like to exercise."

"I'm giving you a ride home," Charlotte decides, "and you're coming over for dinner. Pack up so we can make it home before Jenny whines about us being late."

"Do I have a choice in any of this?" Kyle asks, even as he saves his work and closes his computer. He'll make a few adjustments to the draft on the left and send them both to his client. Someone else can make the final decision.

"We'll stop at the store on the way home. You can choose what we're having for dinner."

"I get it now," Kyle says, laughing. "You're inviting me over as a clever ploy to make me cook for you."

"I don't need clever ploys for that. I just need to ask." She smiles at him as she tucks her glasses away into their case. "Do you want to make dinner for us tonight?"

"I would love to," Kyle answers.

CHARLOTTE WAS RIGHT. She doesn't need tricks to make Kyle cook for her or even to lure him over for dinner. What she *does* need tricks for is to make him willingly walk into an ambush. Kyle's too caught up in figuring out what toppings they need to make baked potatoes into a meal by themselves to realize the promise of cooking was the bait instead of the goal.

"So," Jenny says after the potatoes are in the oven and Kyle's committed to being here for another hour to keep an eye on them. "I heard you were seen leaving Enchanting Encounters this morning. Did you have a fun night?"

"Uh," Kyle says, stalling, then his phone buzzes, offering him the perfect distraction.

Aidan: *I didn't have a chance to text you between classes. How are you feeling?*

Okay, maybe this isn't the best distraction. Kyle glances up to confirm both women are watching him closely, and he leans against the counter, aiming for casual as he texts Aidan back.

Kyle: *Good. I did some work and now I'm making dinner. You good?*

Aidan: *Yes. I was pleasantly distracted throughout the day. I'd like to meet up tomorrow to talk about last night's scene.*

Kyle: *And plan the next one?*

Kyle thinks about adding a smiley face, but that seems like it's pushing it.

Aidan: *Yes.*

It's just one word, but it brings a smile to Kyle's face. An obvious smile, he learns, as he looks up from his phone to see both Jenny and Charlotte with their arms crossed over their chests and expectant looks on their faces. So much for playing that conversation as casual.

"Definitely a fun night," Charlotte says.

"Maybe I don't want to talk about it." Kyle slips his phone back into his pocket and washes his hands so he can cut the chicken into thin strips.

"You always want to talk about it," Jenny says.

"Was it not a good night?" Charlotte asks, and that's unfair because she's playing the *concerned* card. Well, since it's Charlotte she's not playing, she actually is concerned, and it makes Kyle feel guilty.

"The scene was great," Kyle says. "The stuff around it..." He makes a so-so motion with his hand. And then because he's terrible at keeping his thoughts to himself he adds, "He stayed the night, which was good until it was weird. Post-scene cuddling is great, but then there's the awkwardness of how far the cuddling can go. Can you kiss? Probably not. Can you nuzzle their neck? Can you hug each other? How long until the cuddling stops and you're just two guys sharing a bed for the night?"

"Idiot," Jenny says fondly. She comes up behind him and presses a kiss to his cheek. "You could try *asking.*"

"I don't want to come across as needy," Kyle says. He wants Aidan to like him. He wants Aidan to keep scening with him which means Kyle needs to put his best self forward.

Jenny smacks him on the back of the head, not hard enough to hurt but not soft enough to be friendly.

"Sorry," Kyle says. He'd rub his head, but he's dealing with raw chicken, and that seems like a bad idea.

Jenny rubs it for him. "If he doesn't like you the way you are, then he's not worth scening with again. I know you know that because you're the one who told me." Her hand stills in his hair. "Did you scene with Aidan last night?"

Kyle is the worst at secrets. He doesn't even know why he tries.

"Wow," Charlotte says. "Congrats."

"Yes, yes, good on you for getting your man," Jenny says. "Can we go back to the part where you didn't tell us?"

"It's just a trial period." He adds the cut chicken to the skillet. "I didn't want to get anyone's hopes up."

"Idiot," Jenny says again, still fond. "So, it wasn't everything you were hoping it would be?"

"It was even better," Kyle says. He slips away from Jenny so he can wash his hands. "But I still want *more.* I don't just want to scene with him."

"You want to kiss him in the morning before he goes to work," Charlotte guesses.

"Feelings?" Jenny asks. "After one scene?"

"Two," Kyle admits and holds his hands up when Jenny looks like she's going to yell at him. "One on the phone, one in person. It's a trial period. I would've told you if we made it more official."

"Did he really stay the whole night?" Charlotte asks.

A smile tugs at Kyle's lips. "Yeah. After the scene on the phone, I mentioned that the worst part about phone scenes is the lack of cuddling, so he packed an overnight bag so he could stay the whole night after our scene if I wanted it."

"I don't think you have to worry about feelings being a problem," Charlotte tells him.

Kyle shrugs. "He's hard to get a read on. I think he's just a nice guy. And a good Dom. He wants to make sure he does things right. That doesn't necessarily mean feelings."

"When are you seeing him next?" Jenny asks. "Is that who you were texting earlier?"

"Yes and no, you can't come. We're going to talk about last night's scene and maybe sketch out our next one."

"You're moving fast," Jenny says.

"Like I said, it's a trial period. We're trying to make sure we're compatible. It makes sense to fit in a bunch of scenes." Also, it's the only guaranteed two weeks Kyle has with Aidan, so he wants to make sure he gets as much out of it as he can in case it doesn't work out.

Charlotte's eyeing him as if she knows the direction his thoughts are heading.

"How did Kids' Corner go?" he asks because work is always a good distraction.

Charlotte stares at him for a long moment before she answers, letting him know that she knows what he's doing and is letting him get away with it.

KYLE SHOWS UP at Enchanting Encounters on Friday night in an outfit he'd wear if he was picking up. It's tight-fitting and shows off his best features, and he doesn't even pretend he's not looking for attention as he wanders over to where Aidan's sitting at the bar.

He waves at a few people, blows kisses to a couple of others, and he even lets Alexa reel him in with the kind of appraising look which makes a blush rise in his cheeks.

"Looking good tonight," she tells him.

"I look good every night."

Alexa curls her fingers around the hem of his T-shirt, and there's an offer in the touch and hunger in her gaze, and if it were any other night, then Kyle would probably take her up on it. But tonight isn't any other night, and Kyle has someone waiting for him.

"I can't," Kyle says and the regret in his voice is real.

"Shame," Alexa says and drops her hand. "Let me know next time you're free."

"Of course."

When Kyle reaches the bar, Aidan has a small furrow in his brow.

"Just because they can't play doesn't mean they can't look," Kyle says as he drags his bar stool closer to Aidan's. It means they're close enough for their legs to touch when Kyle sits down, and Aidan looks down at where their legs are tangled together then at the smirk on Kyle's face, and he shakes his head.

"I'm not jealous or possessive by nature, but you make me want to be."

Kyle grins and leans forward. "Yeah? What other things do I make you want to be?"

"Please spare my ears and wait to answer for another five minutes," TJ says, leaning on the bar counters. "What can I get you two to drink?"

"Rum with a bit of Coke splashed in," Kyle says because he and Aidan already agreed tonight was for talking only. "And a straw."

"Shameless," TJ says. "And you, Aidan?"

"Beer, please. Whatever you have on tap."

"You know what else you could have on tap?" Kyle asks.

TJ groans and leaves to pour their drinks.

"Is this how you're going to be all night?" Aidan asks and he tries to sound annoyed, but he's smiling too much to pull it off.

"You said no to my favorite Friday activities which means the only thing left to me is flirting. Just wait until we move to a booth. It'll be much easier to sit on your lap then."

When TJ returns with their drinks, Aidan eyes Kyle's tall glass of soda.

"I hope there's more than a splash of Coke in there."

Kyle laughs. "Yeah, that's just code for me not scening tonight. TJ knows how much rum to put in. Come on, let's find a booth."

Friday nights are packed, but they find a two-person booth tucked far away in the back corner. It means they won't be noticed, which would be more of a problem if Kyle was here for a social visit. But this thing with Aidan is still new enough Kyle wants to keep it to himself, so this is the perfect place.

Kyle slides the table closer to one side to make room for him to plop himself down on Aidan's lap, sitting sideways so he can see Aidan but not straddling him because that's more than Kyle wants to tease himself tonight.

"I don't know why I thought you were joking about this," Aidan says. He wraps an arm around Kyle's waist, so he can't be too unhappy.

Still, Kyle says, "I can move if you want."

Aidan tightens his hold. "I like you here."

"Good. Me too." He picks his soda up and catches the straw between his lips and makes sure he's grinning at Aidan when he takes his first sip.

"Is this what I have to look forward to tonight? An attractive man on my lap who insists on fellating his straw?"

"We're talking about our next scene," Kyle reminds him. "Consider this my way of giving you a few ideas."

Aidan laughs and takes a sip of his beer. "Are you sure this isn't your revenge because I said we're waiting to scene again until tomorrow?"

"Nah, this is foreplay. My revenge will be when I leave you a voicemail tonight of me jerking off and making you wish you were in my bed with me."

Aidan whispers in Kyle's ear, "And if I tell you I don't want you to come until our scene tomorrow?"

Kyle leans in, his turn to whisper. "I can work with that."

Aidan clears his throat. "So, what you're saying is I shouldn't pick up when you call me later tonight."

"Definitely don't pick up." Kyle nuzzles at the smooth skin of Aidan's neck, and he wants to kiss the same spot, maybe bite a little, but he's not sure if it's okay. Then he remembers Jenny telling him to just ask and, as always, Jenny is right.

"So, what are the rules for when we're not in a scene?" Kyle asks. "Can I kiss you?"

Aidan turns Kyle's head so they're looking at each other. "You have no problem climbing into my lap, but you're asking if you can kiss me?"

Kyle shrugs. He never said his brain was logical. Or, at least, his logic isn't necessarily the same as everyone else's. Because climbing into Aidan's lap, sucking at his straw, promising phone calls later, that all falls under flirting. Kissing is on the next tier.

"You can kiss me," Aidan answers.

He leans against the booth and his arms fall to his sides, opening himself up to whatever Kyle wants. It's a lot to offer, and Kyle certainly won't turn it down. Now, he moves so he's straddling Aidan, one knee on either side of him. He sets his drink down so he can rest his hands on Aidan's shoulders and he brushes their lips together. It's a kiss only by the barest definition of the word and when Kyle pulls back, his lips tingle, wanting more.

He rises up on his knees, which gives him the height advantage then he leans down to kiss Aidan again. This one is deeper, and Kyle's surprised when Aidan doesn't immediately take it over.

Instead, he stays relaxed, his hands now on Kyle's waist, head tipped up for Kyle to kiss however he wants. Knowing he has time, Kyle kisses Aidan slowly, more of an exploration than anything with purpose. He brings his hands up to cup Aidan's cheeks and he's gentle as he kisses the corner of Aidan's mouth before kissing him on the lips again.

It's the kind of kissing that makes Kyle's heart flutter, that makes him want more and to draw the moment out even longer. If they were in a scene or at least somewhere more private, then Kyle might give in to the restlessness building under his skin, but given where they are, he keeps things tame.

When he finally pulls back, it isn't because he's had enough but because he doesn't want Aidan to push him away. Best to stop before he's satisfied than be stopped.

"You like that," Aidan says, surprised. He rubs his thumb across Kyle's bottom lip, plump from all the kissing they've done.

"I do, and we haven't done much of it. It's hard to kiss over the phone. And the last scene..." Kyle lifts a shoulder as if to convey *you shoved me up against the wall and fucked me which was amazing but didn't lend itself to kissing.*

"Is it something you want tomorrow?" Aidan asks. He brushes his fingers over Kyle's cheeks, his touch feather light. "I was rough with you on Wednesday. We could do something gentler."

"You want to hold my hand and tell me I'm pretty?" Kyle laughs. "I don't need that."

Aidan tilts his head to the side, considering, and it makes Kyle squirm in his lap. "But you want it."

Kyle blushes all the way to the tips of his ears and this close, there's no way to hide it.

Aidan runs his hands through Kyle's hair. "You are full of surprises."

"Good surprises?"

"Yes." Aidan runs his hands through Kyle's hair again, and Kyle tips his head into the touch. "We should talk about our last scene before we plan the next one."

"I liked it," Kyle says, "but I still haven't seen you come. Or seen you naked."

"Is that a problem?"

"I'd like to."

"I'll keep it in mind."

Which isn't a guarantee. Kyle twists to pick his Coke up off the table. He doesn't put on a show, not now that they're down to business. "I liked how you made me ask for everything."

Aidan grins, pleased with himself. "I noticed."

"What about you?" Kyle asks. "What'd you like? Or not like?"

"I like it when you're vocal. I really liked when you asked me for things. Watching you struggle with yourself when you wanted something but didn't want to have to ask was, uh, it was a highlight of the night."

It's Aidan's turn to blush, and Kyle brushes his thumbs across the pink skin. "You like making me work for what I want?"

"Yes."

Aidan's watching him with heat in his gaze, and it makes Kyle lick his lips and wish they hadn't taken any kind of scene off the table for tonight.

"I don't usually mesh that well with someone in our first scene," Kyle admits.

Aidan smiles, pleased. "It bodes well for a future." His smile dims a fraction. "If we choose to move forward. I don't want to pressure you."

"I think we make a good team," Kyle says, words slow, measured. He's not sure what spooked Aidan, but he doesn't like it. He wants him relaxed and happy again. "I don't think that'll change, but we can wait to talk about the distant future. Right now, we're talking about tomorrow night."

"Yes," Aidan agrees. "You want to be romanced."

Kyle makes a face even though that's exactly what he wants.

"Do you want to play coy?"

"I'm not that good an actor."

"Which means I'm the one holding us back. I can work with that. I'm sure you'll make it difficult for me."

"I can be very persuasive."

"I've gotten that impression." Aidan tugs at the hem of Kyle's T-shirt. "Will you wear something with buttons?"

"You're going all out, aren't you?" Kyle asks. He likes the idea of Aidan putting this much thought into their scenes and wanting to plan them just right, but he's also sure that in the moment he'll be annoyed when it takes Aidan ten minutes to unbutton his shirt.

"We're on our way home from our first date," Aidan says, and he rests his hands on Kyle's thighs as he spins out their backstory for the scene. "It was dinner, obviously."

More roleplay, but Kyle doesn't mind because in both these scenes he's played someone pretty close to himself.

"Very traditional," Kyle says.

"I'm a traditional kind of guy. We'll start the scene when I'm walking you to your door."

"And my job is to tempt you inside? I'm liking where this is going."

Aidan laughs as he takes a sip of his beer. "You may not like where it ends."

"Nah," Kyle says, looking Aidan over. "I trust you."

Aidan smiles, soft, and presses a kiss to the corner of Kyle's mouth before they run through the rest of the scene.

Chapter Eleven

SATURDAY NIGHT FINDS Kyle in his bathroom, fussing with his hair and shimmying to some pop song while he prepares for his night.

"Hey," Jenny says, popping into his bathroom. "I knocked, but no one answered. You probably couldn't hear me over this racket."

"A man's allowed to play whatever music he chooses in his own apartment," Kyle says. "Keep your country crap in your own."

Jenny laughs as Kyle adds more product to his hair. He's aiming for a casually disheveled look which probably doesn't fit the theme of their scene, but he doesn't care.

"Your hair doesn't match your outfit," Jenny tells him.

He scowls at her through the mirror. He's in a nice-ish pair of slacks and a button-down that he even ironed for the occasion. He tugs at the collar of his shirt. It feels like it's choking him and not in the good way.

"I like my hair," Kyle says.

"It's a Saturday night, so you don't have a client meeting." She leans against the doorway, making herself at home. "Are you going on a date?"

"You sound surprised. My feelings are hurt."

"What happened to your trial period? Aidan's okay with you dating on the side?"

This is how misunderstandings begin, the kind of misunderstandings that lead to screaming matches and punches being thrown—and being banned from bars—so Kyle decides to cut this off before Jenny's imagination can run away with her.

"Aidan and I have a scene tonight. He's taken trial period to heart and wants to show me a spectrum of things we can do. We went rough last scene so now..." Kyle gestures to himself.

"You're going to dinner?" Jenny asks.

Kyle sighs. "Pretending. First date role play."

"Please tell me you're joking."

Kyle runs his hands through his hair again.

"This is a bad idea," Jenny says.

"He wants to *woo* me. Don't you think I deserve to be wooed?"

"I think you're needlessly torturing yourself, but if you two have talked it out and think it's a good idea, then I won't stop you. Where I draw the line, though, is letting you out of the house with your hair looking like *that*."

"No." Kyle brings his arms up to protect his hair. "I look good. Leave me alone."

Jenny taps her foot and waits until Kyle slowly lowers his arms.

"You're giving me a side part, aren't you?" he asks.

Jenny grins.

"I don't know why we're friends."

Jenny pushes his head under the sink and starts over with his hair.

KYLE'S USED TO stares when he walks through the club, but tonight they're more curious than appreciative.

"I think you're in more clothes than I've ever seen you wear," Lou says, one of the few people who approaches him.

"Hilarious."

"Your wrists are covered *and* your ankles," Lou continues with a grin. "Did you find someone with a Victorian kink?"

"I look nice *one time* and everyone gives me shit for it." Kyle nudges Lou toward the bar. "Maybe this is why I don't dress up."

"It's a good look," Lou says.

They find spots at the bar and Kyle glances at Lou, unsurprised to see him in a white button-down with the first few buttons undone to show off pale skin and his collarbone.

"You look like you're picking up tonight."

Lou lights up. Clearly, this was the opening he was looking for. "I'm actually playing with Richard tonight. You had a good time with him, right?"

"He has good instincts, and with a bit of practice, he'll be a really good Dom. You'll have fun."

"He wanted to do something public, but I wanted to hold off until we've done a couple scenes together." He gives Kyle an obvious look. "I don't mind sharing if you want to work something out between the three of us."

"Like a time-share?" Kyle asks with a grin.

Lou matches his grin and shrugs.

"I have something good going right now, but I'll keep it in mind."

"Must be more than good," Lou says. "You never turn down the opportunity to scene in public. And Richard wants to try something more intense than open hand spanking. I bet he'd love to put you up on the Saint Andrew's Cross."

"Tempting," Kyle says because he does enjoy how it makes him feel displayed, "but I'm good."

"Wow," Lou says and his eyes go comically wide.

Before Kyle can turn to see what's caught his attention, someone rests a pair of hands on his shoulders.

"I hope you're not making plans without me," Aidan says.

Kyle grins and leans back until he rests against Aidan's chest. "Never."

Lou's jaw hangs open.

Later, Kyle mouths at him.

"Holy shit," Lou says which isn't even close to subtle. "Uh, congratulations."

Aidan's laugh rumbles through Kyle, and his hands squeeze Kyle's shoulders as he says, "Am I interrupting? I can give you a few more minutes."

"No, we're good," Kyle says.

"We're good," Lou echoes. "Have fun tonight."

"You too."

Aidan slips his hands from Kyle's shoulders, but he makes up for it by holding Kyle's hand. Kyle leans in so their shoulders brush as they walk.

"Did you have a good time?" Aidan asks as they head for the rooms.

Kyle's not sure if Aidan's talking about his conversation with Lou or the pretend dinner they're coming from. He supposes the answer is the same either way. "Yeah, but I'm ready to go home."

"Tired?" Aidan teases.

"Something like that."

Kyle knows what he wants out of tonight, but he has to be careful he doesn't spook Aidan. Knowing the guy, he wants to walk Kyle to the door then kiss his hand and try to leave. Kyle needs to coax him inside. Once they're inside, he can lose some of his clothes, and he's never met a guy who'll walk away from him once he's naked.

They walk by the concierge, Ricky today, and he winks at Kyle as they pass.

"I'm glad your friends approve," Aidan says.

"They think you're good for me."

There's no one else in the hallway right now, and it almost does feel like Aidan is walking Kyle to his apartment. Aidan stops in front of Room Seventeen, and tugs on Kyle's hand when he almost walks right by it.

"Forget where you live?" Aidan asks.

"Distracted." Kyle steps into Aidan's space. He slips a hand into Aidan's back pocket and pulls out the room key. He grins as he scans it and opens the door without having to look away from Aidan. He takes a step back into the room. "Coming?"

"This was our first date. I don't want to rush things."

Kyle takes another step into the room. "You're going to leave without giving me a goodnight kiss?"

Aidan smiles as if he knows what Kyle's doing and doesn't plan on making this easy. "You're the one running away."

"I don't want to give our neighbors a show."

He turns away from Aidan to give him some time to think. He loosens his tie—fuck Jenny for insisting he wear a *tie*—and undoes the first few buttons of his shirt. It's the first time tonight he feels like he can breathe properly, and of course, that's what spurs Aidan into action.

"What're you doing?" Aidan asks.

Kyle turns to see the door shut now, small miracles, but Aidan's frowning at him.

"You sounded like you were leaving so I'm stripping down for bed," Kyle answers. "If you're staying, then you can join me."

Aidan steps closer, and Kyle smiles, sweet except for the way his face must show that all he's thinking right now is how good Aidan will look like once his clothes are gone. Kyle leans in for a kiss, but all he's given is a brush of Aidan's lips against his cheek before Aidan rebuttons his shirt.

"That's the wrong way," Kyle says. "You know that, right?"

"It's our first date, we're taking things slow. I want to do this the right way." Aidan does up the last button of Kyle's shirt. "You deserve that."

Kyle's stomach does something weird and fluttery at Aidan's words, but he ignores it, knocking Aidan's hands away. "I'm losing the tie. It makes me feel like I can't breathe."

"I've felt that way all night." Aidan's gaze is trained on Kyle and his voice is sincere. He lifts Kyle's tie over his head. "Every time I looked at you."

Kyle's mouth falls open. He's an idiot. He's the biggest fucking idiot on the planet. He doesn't know how this scene seemed like a good idea when they were planning it. Maybe because he thought Aidan would play the shy, well-meaning guy for five minutes and drop it as soon as sex was on the table, but that's not where this is headed.

There's no way this doesn't fuck with Kyle's head, and he's not even sure he cares. He summons a smile, one at odds with the sinking feeling in his stomach. "You're a sap. Did I know that when I agreed to go out with you? I don't think I did because that's usually a deal breaker for me."

"Is it a deal breaker now?" Aidan drops Kyle's tie to the floor, but he doesn't move away, his body mere inches from Kyle's.

Kyle wants them closer. They're in a suite, which means they're in the living room now and there's a couch and an armchair and a desk. Through the door is a bedroom, but if Aidan has his way, then they won't make it there until the scene's over.

Kyle will just have to...persuade Aidan to see things his way.

"Kiss me," he says. "You promised."

Aidan leans in to kiss him, their lips the only point of contact between them. Kyle's entire body sways toward Aidan, wanting more. The kiss is chaste, and when Kyle tries to deepen it, Aidan pulls back.

"Good night, then," Aidan says.

"Not a good night," Kyle counters. "Not yet." He wants to bring them back to the bedroom, but he can't risk spooking Aidan. Instead, he takes Aidan's hand and leads him to the couch.

He eases Aidan onto the couch first then straddles him because it'll be harder for Aidan to run away if Kyle's sitting on him.

"I think this is a little fast, "Aidan says, and the concern in his voice is enough to make Kyle pause for a moment.

He wants this, Kyle reminds himself. *He wants* me. *The reluctance is part of the scene. I'm not pressuring him into anything he doesn't want.*

"We're sitting," Kyle says, soothing. "We both have our clothes on."

"You're sitting on me."

Kyle laughs. "Yeah, I am. You feel good." He rolls his hips, a gentle gyration, nothing demanding, just showing Aidan one of the ways he can make him feel good. "How do I feel?"

Aidan blushes, which is fucking commitment to his part. "Good. This isn't the first time I've had an erection, you know."

"I hope not." Feeling daring, Kyle rolls his hips again. "Does that mean you know what to do from here? I have a few ideas if you don't."

"I know what to do, and I know what I want to do, but that's different from what I *should* do."

"If I want this and you want this, then I don't see why you're fighting it so hard."

"It's our first date."

Kyle rolls his eyes. "You have a schedule to follow? A quick kiss after our first date, maybe you'll slip me some tongue after our third? It's our relationship, we should decide how we do things."

Indecision is warring on Aidan's face, and as much as Kyle wants to grind down on his lap again or kiss him breathless, he doesn't. He remains still, his legs splayed on either side of Aidan's waist, and *waits*.

"My way," Aidan finally says.

"I thought we were compromising."

"We are." Aidan drops a hand between them so his knuckles can graze the growing bulge at the front of Kyle's pants. "You'll get what you want, but you'll get it my way."

"Do you know what I want?"

Aidan grins. "You're a man who spent all dessert licking his spoon more than necessary. I have a good idea of what you want."

Kyle drops his gaze to Aidan's lap, and he doesn't try to hold back the longing in his stare or the way his tongue darts out to wet his lips. "Yeah?"

"Patience." Aidan pats Kyle's hip. "Lie down on the couch."

"Getting me horizontal?" Kyle asks. "We're definitely not going slow anymore."

"Are you trying to talk yourself out of mutual orgasms because that's what it sounds like you're doing right now."

Kyle mimes zipping his lips. He gives it about a minute before he runs his mouth again. He slides off Aidan's lap, and Aidan shifts forward so Kyle can stretch out across the couch. Honestly, Kyle's surprised they're not using the bed for their "first date" sex. He expected the bed with the lights off, but he doesn't want to say anything in case he loses his chance to see Aidan naked.

Aidan moves between Kyle's legs and bends down to kiss him. Kyle arches up into the kiss, half-afraid Aidan will pull away again. When he doesn't, Kyle pushes his luck a little more, sliding a hand up Aidan's spine until his fingers are curled around the back of his neck. He pulls Aidan closer and breathes a sigh of relief when Aidan goes with the touch instead of fighting it.

Aidan lowers himself down until he's lying on top of Kyle, and he even grinds his hips against Kyle's, which would feel good except... "Belt off," Kyle says.

Aidan props himself up on his elbows, and he looks a little sheepish. "Sorry."

Kyle shrugs. "Happens."

He undoes Aidan's belt and drops it off the side of the couch. Then he eyes Aidan's fly before deciding not to push too much.

"Kiss me again?" Kyle asks.

Aidan's eyes crinkle at the corners when he smiles. "Always," he says before bracing himself on one arm so he can cup Kyle's chin before he kisses him.

It's a soft kiss, and for a moment Kyle believes this is the first time they've ever kissed. It feels that way—gentle, coaxing—almost enough to make him forget that Aidan fucked him up against a wall just a couple nights ago.

But Kyle does remember the other night, and suddenly this kiss isn't enough. He tries to deepen it, but Aidan pulls back. Kyle chases him, snatching a kiss here and another there until they're both sitting up and Kyle's clinging to Aidan's shirt to keep him from moving even further away.

"Slow," Aidan reminds him.

"Fuck slow," Kyle says, a bit of real frustration slipping into his voice. "I want *you*."

Aidan pauses, and Kyle presses his advantage.

"Please," Kyle says. He undoes the first button on Aidan's shirt. "I'll be good for you, I promise. Let me do this."

He manages to undo three buttons before Aidan covers Kyle's hands with his own. Kyle groans and almost thunks his head against Aidan's shoulder when he spies a glimpse of an undershirt under Aidan's button-down.

"You wear too many clothes."

"You're very tempting," Aidan says.

"Then take what I'm offering you."

Aidan groans and pushes Kyle down on the couch, the roughest he's been all night. He immediately follows it up with scattered kisses across Kyle's face then his neck.

"Sorry," Aidan says as if Kyle doesn't have bruises on his hips from the last time they were together.

Aidan's hands stroke over Kyle's wrists, a plea for forgiveness for holding them captive earlier. Kyle would appreciate the touch more if it was skin-on-skin, but Aidan skims his fingers over the stiff cuffs on Kyle's shirt.

"Please," Kyle says. He's not even sure what he's asking for.

Aidan takes one of Kyle's wrists in both of his, and he undoes the cuff buttons and rolls Kyle's sleeve back once to reveal his wrist. Aidan dips his head to press a kiss against the thin skin covering the inside of Kyle's wrist.

Kyle doesn't realize he's trembling until Aidan lets go and reaches for his other wrist.

"What're you doing?" Kyle asks.

The fluttery feeling is back in his stomach, and now it's his turn to want to pull away.

"Has no one ever done this for you before?"

Kyle shakes his head, unsure whether he's answering as himself or whatever construct of himself he's supposed to be in this scene. His breath stutters out as Aidan's lips graze the skin of his other wrist.

"They should have," Aidan says. "You deserve it."

Aidan undoes the button of Kyle's collar, parts his shirt so he can lay a kiss there, as well, just at the hollow of his throat. Kyle's eyes slip closed, and he holds his breath, afraid to break whatever spell Aidan's weaving around him.

"You're so beautiful when you trust me," Aidan says.

Kyle's eyelashes flutter, but his eyes stay closed, and Aidan lays a kiss on one eyelid then the other.

"I spent all dinner thinking how lucky I was to have you sitting across from me," Aidan says, and it takes Kyle an embarrassing amount of time to remember they *didn't* go to dinner before this. "I thought about trying to hold your hand at the restaurant."

"I would've let you." Kyle opens his eyes again and wishes he hadn't. Aidan's braced above him, watching him with something unbearably soft in his eyes. "I'll let you do anything you want to me."

The softness disappears in a blink, and Aidan pulls away before Kyle even realizes he's done something wrong.

Before Kyle can apologize, Aidan runs a hand through Kyle's hair to break up the gel and ruin his side part. "You shouldn't promise that," he says.

Kyle nods. He knows that. There are, in fact, things he won't let Aidan do to him. Things he won't let anyone do.

"Okay," Kyle says because he knows when he's spooked his partner. "Can I show you something I will let you do?" He reaches for Aidan's fly, hoping to get them back on track.

It works, sort of.

Aidan pushes Kyle's hands away, par for the course tonight, really.

"Please?" Kyle asks because he knows Aidan likes it when he's vocal when he asks for the things he wants. "I can make you feel so good."

"I have rules." Aidan tries to sound stern, but he's not putting up as much of a fight as before.

"Aren't I worth breaking the rules for?"

Aidan hauls Kyle in for a kiss that leaves his lips stinging afterwards.

"Fine," he says when they finally pull apart. "You can pick one article of clothing we each lose, but that's it. I'm trying to do the right thing. You deserve more than a quick fuck on the couch after our first date."

"There's a bed in the other room. We can take it slow if that's what you want."

If it means Kyle will be fucked before tonight's over, then he'll agree to doing it any way, but he knows better than to make such an open-ended offer again.

"You can take your time opening me up," Kyle says. "We can even turn the lights off if you're shy. And if you're afraid we're moving too fast, then you don't have to let me come. I just want you in me. Please."

"Do you really think I'd leave you hanging?" Aidan asks. "Is that the kind of lover you think I'd be?"

Lover, Kyle thinks, a little despairingly.

"Are you ready to pick what clothes we're losing?" Aidan asks.

"If I choose your underwear, can I also unbutton your pants?"

"Clever," Aidan says, smiling, "but no."

"If date one means we get to lose one article of clothing, does that mean for date two I can get rid of two?"

"If I say yes, will you only wear jeans and a T-shirt?"

It's easy, maybe a little too easy, to buy into the thought that in a few days they'll go on a date together. Maybe dinner again where they hold hands under the table, and Kyle tries to take his time and pay attention to what Aidan's saying, even though he'll be desperate to take him home.

"You can spend all dinner thinking about how I'm commando," Kyle says.

"I'm thinking about it now. I wonder if your cock is as pretty as the rest of you."

Kyle flushes. "I'm not *pretty*."

"I disagree." Aidan brushes his thumb across Kyle's flushed cheeks. "But I can say beautiful instead if it makes you more comfortable. You didn't object to that before."

Kyle's not sure whether to turn into Aidan's words or away from them. This is what Aidan promised him last night when they planned this scene, but Kyle didn't realize it would hit him quite so hard. He figured Aidan would play it closer to humiliation than genuine.

"Take off your pants," Kyle says because changing the subject seems the best option.

"One date and the romance is gone," Aidan says, but he stands up so he can take his pants off.

Kyle stays on the couch as he shimmies out of his own pants. "You're the one being a tease."

Aidan stands in front of Kyle in a button-down and gray boxer briefs with a damp spot on the front. Kyle wants to lean in and press his lips to the spot or maybe sprawl against the couch like an invitation.

"If I give you everything you want, then I won't have anything left to offer you."

Kyle's not sure if they're still role-playing or if Aidan actually means that. "I doubt you'll be able to give me everything I want in one night. I have a very long list."

Aidan arches his eyebrows.

"And even if you did," Kyle continues, sitting up and hooking his fingers through the waistband of Aidan's briefs, "I would want it all over again. I won't grow bored of you."

Now who's blurring real versus roleplay?

Aidan smiles, bright and brilliant, and then he seems to remember himself. "Is this a ploy to convince me to move into the bedroom?"

"No ploy. You said we're doing this your way, so we're doing it your way."

"You're suddenly very sweet." Aidan sounds suspicious.

"I can be sweet."

"When it suits you."

Kyle shrugs, conceding the point.

Aidan clasps Kyle's hands in his own. At first, Kyle thinks it's because he believes he will try to pull his briefs down, but then Aidan tugs on Kyle's hands until he stands up. They switch places, Aidan sitting down and Kyle standing up.

Another tug and Kyle straddles Aidan's lap like when they first sat on the couch tonight, except now they're not wearing pants. *This is much better.* Kyle rocks his hips against Aidan's.

"Please tell me this is okay," Kyle says.

"It is," Aidan says. "It's how you'll come tonight."

"Seeing each other's dicks isn't okay but coming in my briefs is?"

"My way," Aidan reminds him. He drops Kyle's hands so he can curl his fingers around Kyle's hips and pull him flush against his body. "Besides, I know you like it. I can feel it."

Kyle drapes his arms around Aidan's neck and leans in. "I feel like we're slow dancing."

"This is how you dance?"

Kyle grinds his hips down. "Yeah," he says with a smirk. "Are you gonna take me dancing for our next date?"

"We might have to hold off on it for a bit. Maybe date four."

"Right. We're going *slow.*"

Aidan pulls Kyle in for a kiss, which, to be fair, is one of the best ways to shut him up. Kyle presses even closer and tries to remember the last time he made out with someone on a couch like this. He runs his fingers through Aidan's hair and holds on, in case Aidan's entertaining thoughts of breaking the kiss.

Heat builds between their bodies, and Kyle wishes, again, that he was in a T-shirt and not this stupid long-sleeve button-down. He's sweating through it, and it makes him feel overheated and overdressed as he rocks his hips against Aidan's.

His pleasure grows in stages, need pooling in his belly, want making him chase the taste of Aidan's mouth. This should feel ridiculous, kissing and grinding on the couch. It should be something he outgrew years ago, but this is what Aidan's giving him, and he's already established he'll take anything Aidan offers.

Eventually, Kyle has to break the kiss as he breathes heavy against Aidan's neck and chases an orgasm that's just out of his reach. Maybe he *is* too old for this.

"Are you close?" Aidan asks. His palm is hot as it slides down Kyle's back, and Kyle presses back into the touch.

He nods. He's close but—

"Do you need more?"

Kyle nods again.

Aidan slides his hand down to Kyle's ass. He urges Kyle to grind against him harder, faster. Kyle does, even though all he's doing is pushing himself closer to an edge he won't be able to tip over. He resists against the urge to bite down on Aidan's neck. He presses open-mouthed kisses against the skin instead as he pants and growls and works himself up more and more.

"Please," Kyle begs. He's so close. All he needs is for Aidan to bite him or yank on his hair or do *something* to spark his orgasm. He can feel the hard line of Aidan's cock every time he grinds his hips, and it would be so easy to shove their briefs down and wrap a hand around their dicks.

His hand drifts down like he's thinking about it but then he curls his fingers around Aidan's shoulders instead. He wants to be good, and Aidan said their clothes were staying on.

"Please," Kyle says again.

"Shh," Aidan tells him. "I've got you."

Aidan's hands squeeze Kyle's ass cheeks then spreads them the best he can.

Kyle presses his mouth against the back of his hand to stifle his pleas because Aidan doesn't want to hear them. He promised Kyle he'll take care of him, and Kyle needs to trust him. He—

Oh, Kyle thinks as Aidan's finger presses against his hole. Kyle can feel the touch, the promise there even through his briefs. He digs his teeth into the skin of his hand and tears spring into his eyes because this isn't going to be enough. This is another tease in a long line of them, and Kyle can only take so much before he breaks.

"I want you to come for me," Aidan says, his words spoken against Kyle's ear. "Can you do that for me?"

Kyle shakes his head because he can't. Except he can, he *does*, and his body shakes apart, only held together by Aidan's steady grip on him. He slumps against Aidan's chest when he's done, sweating and panting and exhausted by the effort it took for him to come.

Aidan rubs his hands soothingly up and down his back.

It takes a long time before Kyle lifts his head from Aidan's shoulder. He's loose, but still not quite settled.

Aidan kisses him again, Kyle's mouth soft and pliant against Aidan's more insistent one. It's a nice change, for Aidan to be the one desperate instead of Kyle. Then he shifts on Aidan's lap and feels the press of Aidan's cock and—*oh*.

Aidan hasn't come yet.

The desperation makes more sense now, and Kyle breaks the kiss so he can slide off Aidan's lap and to the floor where he kneels between Aidan's legs. There's a damp spot on Aidan's briefs, and he can see the hard line of Aidan's cock, and it's the closest Kyle's been to seeing it since they started this thing together.

He dips his head so he can kiss Aidan's hard length and he trails his lips lower, to the soft, heavy press of his balls. It feels weird to do this with Aidan's briefs in the way, but Kyle knows better than to think Aidan will change his mind about that now. And he's nothing but creative when it comes to getting what he wants.

He can still breathe heavy against Aidan, can still press kisses along his cock. And, maybe if Kyle shows how good he is at this then next time Aidan will give him the chance to suck him properly. Or maybe, if Kyle's really lucky, he can make the case for it now.

He glances up at Aidan, his fingers on the waistband of Aidan's briefs. He doesn't tug them down, doesn't even hook his fingers through the waistband because he doesn't have permission. But Aidan's cheeks are flushed and his hands are restless in Kyle's hair, and maybe he'll give up on his stupid rules.

Then Aidan shakes his head. "I thought I was going to kiss you and go home. I didn't bring condoms with me."

It's a fucking *lie,* and even if it wasn't, there are condoms stashed all around the suite, but that isn't the game they're playing.

Kyle whines a little, and maybe he'll be embarrassed by it later, but right now, all he wants is Aidan's dick. He wants it in his ass, his mouth, his hand, he doesn't care. He just wants it. He dips his gaze down, considering if Aidan will let him blow him through his briefs.

A sharp tug of his hair gives him his answer.

"Tell me," Aidan says. He holds Kyle at bay with a hand tight in his hair while his other hand cups his cock. He squeezes his balls then drags the heel of his palm against his shaft and Kyle squirms, partly to feel the sharp spike of pain where he's held and partly because he knows where this is headed.

"I want it so bad," Kyle says, his voice raspy as if he'd been able to suck Aidan's dick. "I would make it good for you. All I want is my mouth on you. Will you let me?"

"How desperate are you?" Aidan asks.

He holds Kyle back as he touches himself, and his hips get in on the action, rolling into his hand.

Kyle's not sure whether to stare at Aidan's hand or his mouth. His gaze darts between both, settling on Aidan's face when he says, "Please," low and needy.

Aidan's eyes are dark, glittering, as he stares down at Kyle. "What if I slapped your face with it?"

"Yes," Kyle breathes. He wants to ask where the nice man who took him to dinner and insisted on all their clothes staying on went, but he doesn't want Aidan to stop. He wants him to follow through. "I'd take it and beg for you to do it again."

Aidan groans and the hand in Kyle's hair slides down so he can trail his fingers across Kyle's cheek as if he's imagining it.

"I'd let you slap me with your cock," Kyle says. "And when you were done using me like that, I'd open my mouth and let you use me another way."

Kyle's the one to break eye contact, and he dips his gaze down to Aidan's cock. "Please let me. I'd make it so good for you. I—"

Aidan slides his fingers into Kyle's mouth, cutting off what he was going to say, and Kyle sucks them the way he wants to suck Aidan's dick. He shows Aidan how good he is with his mouth. He nips at the tips of Aidan's fingers, and when he takes them deep, Aidan groans and presses his hand against his dick.

His hips jerk up and his fingers press down against Kyle's tongue, his body tensing up before he slumps against the couch. He breathes heavily, still staring at Kyle, even as he slips his fingers out of Kyle's mouth.

"That's not what I had in mind for our first date," Aidan finally says. He wipes his fingers on Kyle's cheek, leaving a trail of spit behind.

"Tease," Kyle says, fond but also a little serious. He glances down at Aidan's lap and the noticeable wet spot because if they committed, then they could still make Kyle's hopes for the night come true.

"Not tonight," Aidan says. "Maybe next time."

Kyle sits up higher on his knees. "Can I?"

Aidan looks confused, but he nods anyway, and Kyle climbs back into his lap. He doesn't mind being on the floor, but right now he needs to be close. He blames it on the premise they set for tonight. He wants to tuck himself under Aidan's chin or curl up on the bed with him. He wants soft touches and softer whispers, and he's not sure what he's allowed to have.

He's leaning in for a kiss when he pauses, uncertain. "Is this it? Are we done?"

"You can kiss me." Aidan draws Kyle in for a lingering, sweet kiss, none of their earlier urgency in it. When Aidan pulls back, it feels too soon. "We should shower."

"Yeah, scene's definitely over if you're suggesting we get naked together."

Aidan laughs and runs a hand through Kyle's hair, pushing it off his forehead. "You can have the first shower."

"Is this a thing? I feel like that's something you have to warn a guy about."

"It's not a thing," Aidan answers. "Well, it wasn't. It might be now. I don't think you understand how fun it is to wind you up."

"Ugh," Kyle says, but there's no real heat in it. He kisses Aidan, a quick press of lips. "I'm going to use all the hot water when I shower."

"That would be impressive."

Kyle stands up and evaluates the state of his briefs—wet and sticky and uncomfortably cool—and his button-down, which is wrinkled beyond salvaging. He eyes Aidan who's rumpled but not quite as badly.

"I have a change of clothes in my locker," he says. "Can you grab them for me while I'm in the shower? I don't go commando in dress pants, and I'm putting serious thought into burning this shirt."

Aidan laughs. "I can get your clothes for you."

He pulls his pants on over his come-damp briefs, and he makes a face as he zips up, but he doesn't complain. Kyle reels him in before he can take more than two steps toward the door. He kisses Aidan one last time, messing up his hair while he does it, and pulls Aidan's dress shirt out of his pants. When Aidan draws breath to protest, Kyle slips him a little tongue and backs him up against the wall to kiss him harder.

When Kyle's done with him, Aidan looks freshly fucked. The only thing that could make it better would be if Kyle left a hickey or two on his neck, but this will still work.

"There," Kyle says, stepping back to admire his work. "Now everyone knows you're off-limits."

"I'm coming back to you," Aidan promises. "I'm just tracking down some clothes first."

"Extra insurance," Kyle says. He unbuttons his shirt and throws it at the couch with a grin, glad to finally be rid of it. "Can I jerk off?"

"Are you asking because you want me walking around with a semi because of you or because you want me to tell you what to do?"

"It can't be both?"

It's Aidan's turn to pull Kyle in for a kiss. When he pulls back, Kyle sways toward him, wanting more, but Aidan holds him at bay. "You can touch yourself as much as you want, but you can't come."

"Okay."

"And drink something while I'm gone."

Kyle rolls his eyes. "You'll be gone for five minutes. But yes," he says as Aidan narrows his eyes. "I'll drink something while you're gone."

He wanders into the bedroom and takes a juice out of the mini-fridge. He waves it at Aidan as evidence before bringing it into the bathroom with him. Shower juice isn't quite as good as shower beer, but it'll do.

And once he's clean and in fresh clothes, he can climb into bed with Aidan, and that'll be even better.

Chapter Twelve

KYLE WAKES UP to Aidan's alarm again, but this alarm isn't as obnoxious as the last one, which is something small to be grateful for. It's still loud enough to disturb Kyle's sleep and that makes him slap drowsily at Aidan's shoulder.

"Turn it off," Kyle says. He doesn't open his eyes because he's not willing to give up on sleep yet. "It's *Sunday*."

"Not a morning person?" Aidan asks.

Kyle cracks an eye open because if his options are sleeping or working, then he'll pick sleeping every time, but if his options are sleeping or Aidan then that changes the game. Aidan reaches over to grab his phone and turn his alarm off.

Aidan's hair is more of a mess than it was last night, and he's in his undershirt and a pair of pajamas pants which, sadly, makes this the most underdressed Kyle's seen him.

"Depends on the morning," Kyle answers. "Do you have somewhere you need to be?"

"Here." Aidan smiles, soft and gentle, and it reminds Kyle too much of last night—that was *roleplay*, they're in real life now—and he slides out of bed and away from Aidan's warmth.

"Breakfast?" Kyle asks. "I know a few good places near here."

"I could eat," Aidan says.

Kyle packs away two pancakes, a double order of eggs, and three sausage links in the time it takes Aidan to drink his coffee and poke at his eggs.

"Maybe *you're* not the morning person," Kyle says.

"Guilty as charged."

"Then why the alarm?"

Aidan lifts his coffee cup to his mouth before he remembers he's finished it. He sets it back down, a flush on his cheeks. "I, uh, didn't want to miss you this morning. Sometimes I'm a heavy sleeper."

"I wouldn't sneak out while you're sleeping," Kyle says. "Just, you know, for future reference."

"Does that mean no more alarms unless I have work?"

Kyle grins. "There are much better ways to wake up if we have the time."

Aidan tries to drink out of his empty coffee mug again.

THEY LINGER OVER their breakfast because neither of them wants to leave, but Kyle has a growing pile of weekend chores, and he's sure Aidan has better things to do with his Sunday than push the remnants of his eggs around his plate, so eventually they pay their bill and leave.

But they linger in the parking lot, Aidan walking Kyle to his car and then not leaving. It's sweet, and Kyle smiles and wonders if it's too soon to invite Aidan over to his apartment. Aidan probably won't care that Kyle has laundry to wash and a kitchen to clean and new recipes to try. Maybe Aidan would even stay for dinner.

"You're thinking hard," Aidan says.

"Running through my to-do list for the day."

"Yeah, I have one of those too. During the week, it always seems like a good idea to put everything off until Sunday. Then Sunday comes and I wish I'd done some of it earlier."

"Busy then?" Kyle asks.

"My students aren't very patient. If I don't have their papers turned around in a day or two, they pester me during my office hours."

"Then I should let you go. We'll talk again tomorrow? Maybe try to see each other sometime this week?"

"Yes. If you need anything today, I'm not doing anything more important than you."

"Wow," Kyle says. "Smooth."

Aidan frowns, which means he was being sincere, and Kyle brushes a kiss across his lips to cut off whatever he had to say.

KYLE'S GOOD MOOD lasts for as long as it takes him to drive home. His head is full of pleasant thoughts from last night and plans for their phone call tomorrow and idle fantasies for what he wants for their next scene.

But then he comes home to an empty apartment, and it's nothing different than usual, except today it hits him a little harder. He brushes the feeling away and gathers his laundry and dumps it all in the washer. His clothes from last night go in last, and he hesitates with his hands on the lid of the washer.

It's just my fucking laundry. What the fuck is wrong with me?

He slams the lid down then has to open it again to put in the detergent pod. Slamming it a second time isn't nearly as satisfying. He jams the start button and curls up on his couch with his favorite blanket.

Gentle scenes are more likely to make him drop than rough ones, something he should've remembered *before* agreeing to the scene with Aidan.

He knows he doesn't deserve to have his ass beat when he signs up for a spanking or a paddling. He might want that kind of pain, and his Dom might want it, and they may make up reasons for why it's happening, but at the heart of things, Kyle isn't *bad.*

Unfortunately, it's too easy to believe the same thing after gentle scenes. He might want to hear nice things, and Aidan might want to say them, and yeah, they can use a first date or whatever as a reason to be saying them, but it doesn't mean they're true.

It was just a scene. He didn't mean any of it. If he did, then he wouldn't have left me in the parking lot. Would it be impossible to grade papers here while I did laundry? No. I'm not worth sticking around for.

Kyle reaches out blindly for his phone, and he knocks a book off his coffee table and his fingers close around the remote before he remembers his phone is on the kitchen counter. That's too far away to be worth getting up. And Aidan has better things to do than listen to Kyle whine.

He pulls his blanket over his head and wallows until the washer beeps to tell him the cycle's done. He debates staying where he is on the couch, but it's not good for his clothes to sit wet in the washer. After he switches them to the dryer, he can return to being a lump on the couch.

He switches his laundry. Then because he's already up, he grabs his phone and heads down the hall to Jenny's apartment. He's still not willing to interrupt Aidan's afternoon, especially not so soon after telling him he was fine, but he knows better than to be on his own right now.

He knocks on Jenny's door to warn them he's here then lets himself in.

She and Charlotte are in the living room watching Sunday morning cartoons because Jenny is secretly a child. Maybe intruding on their morning wasn't such a good idea. They're curled up with each other on the couch, Jenny playing with Charlotte's hair while Scooby-Doo investigates his latest mystery.

They haven't noticed him, which means he still has time to leave. He steps back toward the door which, of course, is when Charlotte spots him. She nudges Jenny, who pauses the TV before she looks up.

"Wow," Jenny says when she sees Kyle. "You look like shit."

Kyle shrugs. "Can I hang out with you guys for a while?"

"Of course," Jenny says.

Charlotte pulls her knees to her chest so there's space on the couch, but Kyle takes a pillow and drops it on the floor. He isn't a part of *them,* and he doesn't want to be more in the way than he already is. He lies down near the couch and braces himself for a flurry of questions.

"There's a masked villain," Jenny says, filling Kyle in on the episode.

"There's always a masked villain," Kyle says.

Jenny hits play, and they're silent as they watch the crew try to figure out the mystery of the haunted circus.

Sitting with them, even if they aren't talking, is better than being by himself in his apartment. His bad thoughts are still lurking, waiting to flood his head again, but they stay away while he's with Jenny and Charlotte. It's like his brain knows better than to think stupid shit when Jenny's around. He wishes his brain respected *him* like this.

The episode turns over to the next one, and Kyle sits up to lean against the couch.

"The scene was a bad idea," Kyle says. He pauses, waits for Jenny's *I told you so.* She doesn't say it, even though he wishes she should. He wants to be angry with someone besides himself. "I wanted it to be real, and it wasn't, and my head's all fucked now."

"You can't scene with Aidan again until you talk to him," Jenny says.

"I know, but not right now. Can I stay a bit longer?"

"You can stay as long as you need to," Jenny tells him.

Kyle makes it through another episode before he drifts into the kitchen to make lunch.

"You don't need to do that," Jenny calls to him.

"I know," he calls back. But he wants to, and maybe a little part of him needs to. Jenny would yell at him if he told her he needs to do something for her because she's done something for him so he keeps that part to himself.

He pulls up a recipe on his phone, and he cooks, settling with each ingredient he prepares and each step he follows. He should've done this in his own apartment. He knows this is the best way to comfort himself, and he could've done this without intruding and without worrying anyone.

Stupid. His thoughts continue to torment him.

Charlotte, like some kind of mind reader, wanders into the kitchen to keep him company.

"You should keep watching your show."

"Not all of us feel the need to make up for strict parenting rules by being lazy on Sunday mornings."

"I thought Jenny made up for a childhood of rules with tattoos?" Kyle smiles, and it's fleeting, but it's a start at least.

"Some rebellions never end, I guess." Charlotte comes around to Kyle's side of the island, and she stands near him, but she doesn't offer him a hug or a hand on his shoulder because she knows him well enough to know he's too prickly for that right now. "What're you making?"

"Quiche. You had some leftover ham and broccoli. If that was your lunch tomorrow then sorry."

"I don't like cold ham, and the microwave at the library is broken right now, so this is perfect."

Kyle puts the quiche in the oven and sets the timer. "You didn't have any pie crust, so I had to make the dough out of Bisquick. It'll taste different than it usually does."

"I'm sure it'll be fine," Charlotte says.

Kyle nods and washes all the dishes he used to make the quiche. He dries them to draw out the process a little longer, and once he's put them away, he looks over his shoulder and Charlotte's still standing there.

"You don't need to babysit me," Kyle says, drawing his shoulders up. "Don't you want to watch your show?"

"I've seen this one before. Can you show me that cowboy chili you were talking about the other day?"

"I know what you're doing." Kyle digs their crockpot out of a lower cabinet. "I'm not saying it won't work, but I'm not stupid."

"You aren't," Charlotte agrees and hops up on the counter to watch him gather everything he'll need for the soup.

KYLE DOES THE dishes after lunch, and he's just putting the last plate away when his phone dings on the counter.

Aidan: *Everything all right?*

It's a standard check-in text, the kind Kyle honestly should've been expecting, but it still makes his chest seize up as if somehow Aidan *knows*. He glances up from his phone to see Charlotte and Jenny staring at him.

Kyle sighs. "I know. I need to talk to him."

"I didn't say anything," Jenny says.

"Thanks for lunch and the company," Kyle says. He tucks his phone into his pocket then pulls it back out again. "I'll be by later, maybe."

"If you're not here for dinner then we'll save the chili for tomorrow," Charlotte says.

Kyle nods and ducks out of their apartment.

He calls Aidan once he's in his own apartment, the door shut tight behind him. For the first two rings, he allows himself to imagine that Aidan won't pick up. It would be a good excuse to let this go, regroup, and be better next scene.

Aidan picks up on the third ring, dashing Kyle's hopes. "Good afternoon."

"Hi." Kyle tucks his phone against his ear and takes his clothes out of the dryer. He dumps them in his laundry basket and drags it into the living room to fold.

"How are you doing?"

There's no way Aidan doesn't know the answer to that question, there wouldn't be any reason for Kyle to call instead of texting back if everything was fine, but it's still a struggle for Kyle to answer. "I've been better."

He pulls a white T-shirt off the top off his laundry basket and turns it right-side-in before folding it.

"Do you need me to come over?" Aidan asks. "Or we could meet somewhere neutral if that would make you more comfortable."

"You don't need to do that." Kyle pulls a black T-shirt out. "I'm okay. I was with Jenny and Charlotte earlier."

There's a long silence, enough for Kyle to fold two more shirts before he realizes Aidan isn't saying anything.

"You're mad at me," Kyle says which, duh. He just told him that instead of calling Aidan to help him he went to a different Dom. *Fuck.*

Kyle drops his jeans back into his laundry basket so he can rub his eyes. Is there any way he can get a redo on today?

"I'm not mad at you," Aidan finally says.

"But you're not happy."

"I'm not."

Kyle abandons his laundry and leans against his couch. In a scene when he messes up, he knows how to fix it. He flounders when he messes up in real life. He pulls his knees up to his chest and hopes Aidan will give him a clue.

"I'm your Dom for these two weeks," Aidan says, his words slow, careful, as though he's weighing them before he says them. "You should come to me if you need something. And if you don't think you can, then that's something we need to address."

"I know I can talk to you." Kyle doesn't want Aidan to think he's a bad Dom. He's good enough Kyle wants to keep him even if his brain's trying to sabotage him today. "I just didn't want to be a burden."

It sounds stupid when Kyle puts it like that, and he scowls at himself and says. "All I did was watch TV with them for a bit and made lunch. I didn't—" He didn't kneel for Jenny or ask her to tie him up, things he's had to ask for in the past when he dropped hard and didn't have anyone else to turn to.

It's stupid because this time he has Aidan, and he just didn't pick up the phone.

"You aren't a burden," Aidan tells him. "I'm not angry you dropped or that you went to someone you trusted for support. I'm upset because I haven't made you feel like I can be that person for you."

"I'm fucking this up," Kyle says. He rubs his eyes again. "You haven't done anything wrong. This is all on me. I knew I could've called you, and I almost did, but I only wanted you to see me at my best. I—I want you to like me."

"You think I won't want you if you're not perfect?"

Kyle pokes at his laundry and doesn't say anything for a while. Then because Aidan deserves the truth, he says, "I know I'm a lot of work in scene, so I try not to be out of it. And usually, I'm not." That's the most important thing for Aidan to know. Kyle's not usually this much of a mess after a scene. He wasn't with the other two, and he hopes Aidan remembers that and not just this.

Fuck, he shouldn't have called Aidan. He should've just sent off a flirty text then went on with his day.

This is going to ruin everything.

"I agreed to scene with you," Aidan says, "which means I agreed to look after you when we're in a scene but also when we're out of one."

"Yeah, I'm your responsibility." Kyle knows how scening works.

"You say that like it's a bad thing. Do you think responsibility is a burden to me? If I didn't enjoy being responsible for my subs, then I wouldn't be a Dom."

"I'm sorry."

"Trust is inherent with what we do. I know we're still learning about each other, but I hope in the future you feel like you can come to me."

"I'll try. I'm not always good at this part."

"Is there anything I can do for you now?"

Kyle's kneejerk reaction is to say no and hang up so he can agonize over this conversation, but instead, he does what he wanted to do in the parking lot and probably should've done then. "I still have some things to do around the house. I could put you on speaker, and we can stay on the line for a bit."

"Is that something you want or something you think I want?"

"Both? I'd rather not be on my own right now, and I want to show you I'm trying. And I think you want me to want something, but this will be pretty boring for you. I'm just folding laundry and ironing and maybe cooking."

"I still have a stack of papers to grade. If you don't mind me muttering to myself as I work through them, then I'd like to stay on the phone with you."

Kyle switches his phone to speaker and sets it on the couch next to him. "Can you still hear me okay?"

"I can."

They don't talk much after that. Kyle folds his laundry and puts it away and he irons his shirt and pants from last night and hangs them up. Next, he drifts into his kitchen to figure out dinner because he's already bothered Jenny and Charlotte enough for one day.

Aidan grades his papers and he'll laugh quietly to himself if a student writes something completely wrong, and he'll share when a misspelling makes a sentence unintentionally hilarious but, for the most part, they both go about their own lives with the knowledge that someone is on the other end of the phone call if they need something.

Kyle makes homemade macaroni and cheese for dinner because it's his go-to comfort food, and he's pulling it from the oven when Jenny pokes her head into his kitchen.

Her face lights up when she sees the casserole dish and Kyle rolls his eyes, fond, before saying, "I already made you dinner."

"Charlotte says we have to save the chili until you come over and this looks like you're not coming over."

"You can bring some mac 'n cheese back with you," Kyle says. "Let me grab two bowls."

"I don't understand why you trust me with your bowls and not your Tupperware."

"Because I don't care if you return my bowls. I do care about my Tupperware. Though, on second thought, maybe you should go get your own bowls so you don't have to return anything."

"I'll bring them by tomorrow," Jenny says. "And if I forget then you can pester me when you come over for chili. And you're—are you feeling better?"

"Fine." Kyle glances at his phone, sitting on the island counter, still on speaker. "Better than fine. I'm good?"

Jenny follows his gaze and claps a hand over her mouth. "I didn't realize I was interrupting. Sorry."

Kyle hands two bowls of macaroni to her. "Take these and go. Tell Charlotte she continues to be your better half."

"If I had a free hand then I would flip you off. Good night. Swing by if you need anything."

"Go," Kyle says again. He makes a shooing motion with his hands.

Once Jenny's gone, Kyle pours himself a glass of milk and dishes himself out a bowl of macaroni. "I'm sorry about that," he tells Aidan.

"You have nothing to be sorry for. Was that Jenny?"

"Yeah," Kyle answers, cautious. "We went to school together, became friends when I shared my lunches with her. When she bought her first camera, I was her first model. And that turned into me being her first bondage model, which has turned into being best friends. And then I introduced her to her girlfriend, so she's forever in my debt."

"Charlotte and Jenny seem like good friends to have."

"I'd like you to meet them sometime," Kyle says. "You know, properly, not just a walk by on the phone."

"I'd like that. All this talk of food has made me hungry."

"Do you want me to hang up so you can order take-out?"

"I'd rather heat something up and stay talking to you."

Kyle blushes and shoves a forkful of macaroni in his mouth.

Chapter Thirteen

K*YLE AND* A*IDAN* talk throughout the week, but they don't scene again until Friday night. It's good, it's *really* good, but there's an undertone of desperation to it, as if they both know their trial is almost over, and this could be their last scene together. Or, at least, that's how Kyle feels. He's not sure how Aidan feels.

He'll know tomorrow.

On Saturday, Kyle shows up to Enchanting Encounters half an hour earlier then they decided to meet because he's too restless to wait at his apartment. He sits at a little table in the café and shreds napkins until Aidan shows up.

Aidan's in a pair of cuffed khakis that Kyle shouldn't find as endearing as he does. He's paired the khakis with a striped sweater, and Kyle's not sure what's worse—if this is what Aidan grabbed this morning without thinking or if he put time into assembling this outfit.

Kyle spent almost twenty minutes this morning tearing through his closet. He's in black skinny jeans and a T-shirt nicer than his usual V-necks. It isn't the height of fashion either, but at least he doesn't look fifteen years older than he is.

"Making confetti?" Aidan asks, glancing at the strips of napkin on the table.

"Do you want something?" Kyle nods in the direction of the counter.

"Coffee. You want some?"

The last thing Kyle needs right now is coffee. He shakes his head then tosses his napkin mess in the trash while Aidan orders.

"He wants his coffee to go," Kyle tells Marcia, the woman behind the counter.

"I do?" Aidan asks as Marcia grabs a to-go cup.

"I figured we'd go somewhere with a bit more privacy," Kyle says.

"Private is good," Aidan says.

Once he has his coffee, Aidan follows Kyle back through the café then across the bar until they reach the business side of the club. Kyle pulls open a door to reveal fluorescent lights and offices and a couple of scattered cubicles.

"Huh," Aidan says as he looks around.

"And just like that, all the magic is gone," Kyle says with a half-smile. "The curtain has been pulled back." He leads Aidan down to the third office door and knocks on it before pushing it open. "Hey."

Wanda's behind her desk, a purple headscarf on today that both helps tame her unruly curls and looks good. She has a stack of papers surrounding her laptop and she looks up with a smile for Kyle.

"Please tell me you're here to save me from invoices."

Kyle makes a face. "Definitely not. I do enough of my own. Can we borrow an empty office or a meeting room?"

Wanda glances past Kyle and notices Aidan for the first time. "Hello. Sorry for being rude, Kyle doesn't usually bring me friends."

"He's not for you," Kyle says, reaching a hand back to clasp Aidan's.

Wanda smiles, charmed rather than offended. "Meeting Room B is open if you want to use it. A's being used, and C's still a mess from whoever last used it."

"We won't make a mess," Kyle promises.

"I know. Stop by sometime this week for a business chat? I want to talk about our upcoming promotionals."

"Designs? Or participation?"

"Both."

"I'll message you once I have a look at my schedule, and we'll pick a time," Kyle promises.

He backs out of Wanda's office and pulls the door mostly closed again. "That's Wanda," he tells Aidan as they continue down the hallway. "She owns and runs Enchanting Encounters. She's the best person you'll meet here, besides me."

Aidan laughs. "Modest."

"Do you disagree?" Kyle grins as he opens the door Meeting Room B and tugs Aidan inside with him.

It's the smallest of the meeting rooms with enough space for two tables and a handful of chairs. The whiteboard mounted on the wall doesn't have anything written on it right now, but if Kyle squints, then he can make out a faded lunch order.

Kyle drops Aidan's hand and picks a swivel chair to sit in. He only spins once before he plants his feet on the floor and looks at Aidan expectantly. He wonders if Aidan can hear how fast Kyle's heart is beating.

Now is when he figures out how badly he screwed up last week. He and Aidan are compatible, their interests line up well—at least so far—but maybe Kyle's more work than Aidan wants.

Aidan shuts the door and sits in the chair next to Kyle. He uses his foot to turn Kyle's chair toward him.

They stare at each other for a couple of heartbeats, the silence growing louder as neither of them breaks it.

Finally, Kyle says, "I liked these past two weeks. I'd like to do more with you if you feel the same way."

"I do," Aidan says, and Kyle sinks back into his seat, relieved.

Hurdle one cleared.

Now they just have half a dozen more.

"But there are some things we should talk about before we discuss an extension."

"Yeah," Kyle agrees. "The two-week trial was good for dipping our toes in, but it let me get away with only talking about surface level things, and we should dip a little deeper before we commit to anything longer or more serious."

Aidan can't quite keep the surprise off his face.

"I know I screwed things up last week, and I don't want to do it again. You were right when you said I didn't trust you enough yet to go to you when I needed something. I, uh, I have an easier time handing my body over to scene partners than my feelings, but I know if I want something longer to work between us then I need to work on that trust."

"I think we have a good foundation to build on," Aidan says, "but if we are going to continue, then at least in the beginning, I'd like to establish phone check-ins. I'm not comfortable with texts right now."

"Fair. But before we get too far—" *Before I let myself hope too much.* "—I'm not good at moderation. If we're together, then I'm going to give as much of myself to you as you'll let me, and I know that can be overwhelming for some people. And for others, it's not what they want. I just want you to know that."

"I'm not sure what you mean."

"I don't want to scene only at the club," Kyle says. "I want to open my apartment up as a place we can scene, and your place if you're comfortable with it. I like to talk outside of scenes and outside of planning them. I—" He falters here, unsure how much he wants to reveal.

Aidan's patient, doesn't push Kyle while he thinks through what he wants to say.

"There are people at the club who I scene with on a less formal basis," Kyle goes on. "And when I do, I don't mind being someone to call for a quick, or not so quick, fuck. But when I have a steady partner, if there isn't more than scening then I, uh, start to view myself as just a thing to fuck and my head gets messy pretty fast."

Feelings. I want to have feelings. They don't even need to be returned. Just don't mock me for them.

"I get attached," Kyle elaborates, even as his stomach twists up and his throat threatens to close and cut off any more of his words. *It's better to say this now and see if he walks than let myself believe I can have what I want.* "Not in like a weird way. I mean, if we stop scening together I'm not going to stalk you or anything. But when I'm with someone I want to be with them."

Aidan's quiet when Kyle's done rambling, and Kyle doesn't blame him. He just threw a lot of information at him.

"If we agree to an extension then I would also like to use our homes," Aidan says. "Obviously, there are resources at the club I, at least, don't have at home, but I'd also like to wake up in my own bed, or yours, and know we didn't have to be out by a certain time."

Plus, Kyle can cook breakfast for them. Maybe he can even make dinner while Aidan's teaching and have it ready when he comes home. It's a mundane fantasy, maybe, but it's one Kyle's had for years, and one he's never had a chance to realize.

"And I enjoy talking with you," Aidan continues. "Last Sunday when we were on the phone together was something I'd like to do in person if it's something you'd be interested in. I—" It's Aidan's turn to take a fortifying breath. "I want all of you. I want whatever parts of yourself you're willing to give me."

"Oh," Kyle says because he needs to say something, but he's too off-balance for anything more concrete. This is more than he even let himself hope for. This—this could work between them. This could be the relationship Kyle's been searching for the past few years. "Um, yeah. That's good."

Aidan smiles, but there's something guarded about it. "We haven't gotten to my potential deal breaker yet."

Oh, Kyle thinks. Then, *how bad is it going to be?*

"I didn't bring it up for the trial period because it was only two weeks, and we didn't know each other well, but before we decide on anything more long-term, then you should know I was in a relationship before I moved back here."

This kind of talk, then.

"I'll spare you the details," Aidan says, "but he was new to the scene, and it took me longer than it should've to realize he was doing things he was unsure of or flat-out didn't like because he thought I wanted them."

"Oh, shit," Kyle says. That explains Aidan's mini freak-out Saturday when Kyle offered to let him do anything. "I'll be careful not to trigger you on that. And I'm not new to the scene. I know what I like and what I don't, and I don't let people push me into things I don't want to do."

"I know. You're opinionated and mouthy, which is actually what drew me to you in the first place. I'm not hung up on him, but I still feel guilty sometimes. And I worry I'll mess up again, and sometimes I don't know if I should trust myself with you."

"I trust you with me," Kyle says, and he smiles as Aidan snaps his gaze up to his, surprised. "Two-way street, remember? I know I wasn't great at communicating outside of our scene, but I will work on it, and I'm always honest in scene. I have my stoplights, and I use them if I need them. And just because we're talking about an extension it doesn't mean we need to jump into the deep end. We can take our time building our scenes up until we're both comfortable."

Aidan nods. "I would like that."

Kyle slides his chair closer so he can rest a hand on Aidan's knee. "I've been at this a while. You're only in charge because I let you be. Because I like it. If you doubt yourself, then trust that I know what I'm doing and what I want."

"Last Saturday," Aidan says, and Kyle knew they'd have to talk about this more so he doesn't shy away from the topic.

"I wanted everything you said to be true," Kyle says. "I lost sight of roleplay verses reality and convinced myself you didn't mean anything you said. That in the same way, I don't deserve a spanking for being bad, I didn't deserve any of the things you said to me."

Aidan covers Kyle's hand with his. "I did mean it. Every word."

Kyle flushes and tries to pull away, but Aidan doesn't let him.

"You are beautiful," Aidan says, and he catches Kyle's gaze and doesn't let it go. "And you're funny, and you're *smart*. You keep me on my toes during a scene. You push me to be better, and I want to see what we could be if we spent more time together."

Kyle's face feels as if it must be bright red, and this time when he pulls his hand back, Aidan lets him. "Uh, if we're talking about past relationships and shit then I should warn you that I can only do bondage if my Dom stays in eyesight. Preferably, I like being touched if I'm restrained, but I need to see my Dom and speak to him. Or her."

He was left once. His Dom thought he was being too mouthy, and he shoved a gag in Kyle's mouth and went in the other room where Kyle couldn't see him *to give him time to think about his behavior*. It got really ugly.

Kyle shakes the memories away. "Uh, so that's a thing for you to be aware of."

Aidan's lips are pressed tight together, and there's a dark look in his eyes like he wants to track down whoever did this to Kyle and make him pay for it. It had been a shitty thing to do, and Kyle never scened with the guy again, but it hadn't been malicious in intent. It was supposed to discipline Kyle and it very seriously backfired.

"I guess, related to that," Kyle continues. "Um, I know I have a tendency to run my mouth. If you want me to stop, then tell me and I will. And, I guess going back to your thing, if you need me to clarify if I'm whining or actually don't like something, then you can ask."

"Okay," Aidan says. He looks like he wants to reach out and touch Kyle, but Kyle tucks his arms around himself, unsure if he wants to be touched or hugged right now. He's used to feeling vulnerable and exposed in-scene, but he usually tries to avoid it otherwise.

"Is there anything else we need to cover?" Aidan asks.

"Nothing major. I like leather, but not in a fetish way. My first Dom was into it, so the smell always brings me back to the first time I subbed for someone instead of fooling around. It's not a bad thing, but I figured you should know I'll always think about Devon when I smell leather."

"Leather isn't my thing."

Kyle laughs. "Are you sure? I bet motorcycle boots would go real nice with your pressed khakis."

"Hilarious."

Kyle grins, proud of himself. Then his smile fades as he says, "We should talk about collars. I don't like to wear them. Well—" Kyle frowns because that's not quite right. "I do like them, but they mean something. There's commitment and expectation and a lot of things behind them, so I'll wear one if it's needed for a scene, but I won't wear one casually. If we need something to designate when we're in a scene and when we're not, then I have cuffs I use for that. But collars are special."

"I agree," Aidan says. "Cuffs but no collar. I know you enjoy...showing off. I don't have an exhibition kink, but I wouldn't mind having a drink at the bar while you're wearing your cuffs."

"You don't want excessive PDA, but you want to show me off."

"If we agree to extend," Aidan says.

"I think that's the direction we're moving in," Kyle says, "but if I'm wrong, then now is the time to say."

"You're not wrong. Three months this time?"

"Same as before?"

Aidan nods. "We broached the topic of exclusivity before, but I think we should revisit it. Being exclusive for two weeks is different than three months."

"What's your definition of exclusive? No scening with anyone else? No sex with anyone else?"

"I would like to be the only person you scene with or have sex with."

Kyle has to pause to consider if that's something he can do or even wants to. As attached as he can be to one person, he *can* be casual. What he and Jenny have is casual. What Wanda asks him to do can be casual or more involved depending on what she wants from him and who she wants him doing it with.

"What're you thinking?" Aidan asks.

"A bunch of stuff. This isn't meant to be bragging, but I get around. I have friends I'll scene with if we're looking for the same thing and not finding it, I have a thing with Wanda where I'll do demos or promotions for the club, and I still model for Jenny. I'm okay with letting the first one go. If I'm with you, then I want to be with you. I want to be yours. That means coming to you for something instead of looking for it somewhere else."

Aidan nods.

"When I meet with Wanda this week, I can tell her I'm only offering my business services and not my personal ones for the foreseeable future. We both knew this would come up at some point, so it's not a big deal. Maybe in a couple of weeks, we can talk about doing something together or me still doing some demos. It's not a deal breaker if we decide it's something which won't work for us, but I would like to revisit it once we're on more solid ground."

"Which leaves Jenny."

"Yeah." Kyle's not sure how Aidan feels toward Jenny; if he's still upset Kyle went to her instead of him when he dropped last week or if he sees Jenny as competition. She isn't. She's Kyle's best friend, but she'll never be to Kyle what he hopes Aidan will be. Just like Aidan will never be to Kyle what Jenny is.

"Uh, she's my best friend," Kyle says. "And sometimes she ties me up and takes pictures of me for her website or a photography exhibit or a convention she's presenting at. Afterwards, I have a drink and then go home and jerk off about all the people who'll see the pictures and she goes home to Charlotte. It's something I'd like to keep doing, but I could probably give it up. But if that's what you want, then we'll have to postpone our three-month extension because I owe her a photo session."

"Oh?"

A blush creeps up Kyle's cheeks. "I agreed to let her take pictures in exchange for tying me up at the club a couple weeks ago."

Aidan patiently waits for the rest of the story.

"It was part of my quest to attract your attention," Kyle says. "Which, I would like to point out, did eventually work."

"We're coming back to that later," Aidan promises. "But for now, I don't have a problem with you and Jenny continuing what you do."

"That's all my major things then," Kyle says. "Do you want to go formal with this and sign contracts?"

Aidan's entire face lights up before he visibly reins himself in. "Next time. If we agree on a next time, I mean."

Kyle doesn't push. He has his thing about collars being a mark of *significant* and *important* and maybe contracts are Aidan's thing.

"Well, then," Kyle says and he smiles, playful, and he leans in. "Should we seal it with a kiss?"

Aidan grins and curls his fingers around the back of Kyle's neck so he can reel him in until their lips touch, a faint hint of pressure before Aidan pulls back. He doesn't move far, just enough to break their kiss.

"There," Aidan says. "Agreement sealed."

"That's all you're gonna give me?" Kyle asks, and he doesn't hold back on his pout.

"Nothing else I want to do with you is appropriate for this room, and we promised Wanda we wouldn't make a mess."

Kyle sighs and pushes off Aidan's chair, so he slides back a few feet and out of reach of temptation.

"There are, however, dozens of rooms in the building suited for what I want to do to you," Aidan says.

"And what do you want to do to me?" Kyle flutters his eyelashes, knowing it'll make Aidan laugh.

Sure enough, Aidan laughs before he stands and extends a hand to Kyle. "I want to kiss you until you beg me to fuck you."

Kyle places his hand in Aidan's and stands. "That won't take very long."

"I didn't say I would give in once you begged. Maybe I just want to see how desperate I can make you."

"Well," Kyle says, something warm and hopeful unfurling in his chest. "You'll have three months to hear me beg. Maybe you'll grow tired of it."

"I don't think so." Aidan leans in for another brief kiss before he picks his coffee cup off the table. "Let's get you something to drink and plan out our first scene."

"First new scene," Kyle says, purposefully difficult.

Aidan's eyes narrow, but his smile and his tone are playful as he says, "Something with spanking, I think."

Kyle laughs, loud and delighted, and they leave the meeting room still holding hands.

About the Author

Tamryn studied English and Creative Writing in school but has been writing since she could first hold a pencil. Recently, she's turned her focus toward writing erotica. She enjoys writing stories where sex comes first, then feelings because doing things out of order can be fun.

Tamryn has spent the past few months writing the Daniel and Ryan series with a lovely view of mountains out her window, and she's now searching for a new mountain range to serve as her backdrop as she begins her next project.

Other books by this author

Daniel and Ryan Series

Delayed Gratification

The Start of Something New

Who I Am When I'm With You

Positive Reinforcement

Performance Review

Spa Weekend

Weekend Getaway

Caught In Between

Testing the Limits

Tournament of Champions

Coming Soon from Tamryn Eradani

To Have and to Hold

Excerpt

"I can drive myself tonight," Kyle says as he rummages through his closet for the third time in the past five minutes. Jenny's been here for fifteen, amused as he worked himself into a panic, but now her arms are crossed over her chest, and she's moving into impatient territory as he can't settle on what he wants to wear. "You and Charlotte should head out."

Tonight, Kyle's two best friends, Jenny and Charlotte, are meeting his Dom for the first time.

Kyle's been crushing on Aidan since the first time he saw him at Enchanting Encounters, the kink club he's been frequenting for years now. After he managed to catch Aidan's attention, they had a two-week trial period to see if they were compatible beyond physical attraction.

Now that they've extended their play to a three-month commitment, Kyle figures it's time Aidan met the most important people in his life.

Well, that and Jenny was determined to meet Aidan whether Kyle was there or not, and Kyle doesn't need Jenny scaring him off.

"We're not leaving you behind," Jenny says. She sprawls across Kyle's bed, making herself comfortable.

"Absolutely not," Charlotte agrees, wandering in. She lies down next to Jenny, resting her head on Jenny's stomach. "I'm not sure you'd ever make it."

"Besides, if you drive in with me and Charlotte and we have to leave early then you'll have no choice to catch a ride home with your man."

"Huh," Kyle says. It's a good point. It's a Wednesday night which means Aidan has afternoon classes tomorrow. Maybe he could go home with Aidan. Or have Aidan come home with him. As long as there's bed sharing involved, Kyle isn't picky about whose bed they sleep in.

"Never say I don't do anything for you," Jenny tells him. Then, "Put down that shirt. It's basically see-through."

"It looks good on me," Kyle points out, but he puts the shirt back because it's not appropriate for where they're going. He picks up one of his polos and glances at his small collection of dress shirts. "Is this a date?"

"Ugh," Jenny groans.

"Would it be bad if it was?" Charlotte asks.

"You've already seen each other naked," Jenny says. "This can't be more intimidating than that."

"We haven't actually seen each other naked," Kyle says. That is something he's going to change as soon as possible. "And you're trying to distract me. Scenes are scenes and dates are dates. They're different."

"Put a damn shirt on so we can go," Jenny says.

Also Available from NineStar Press

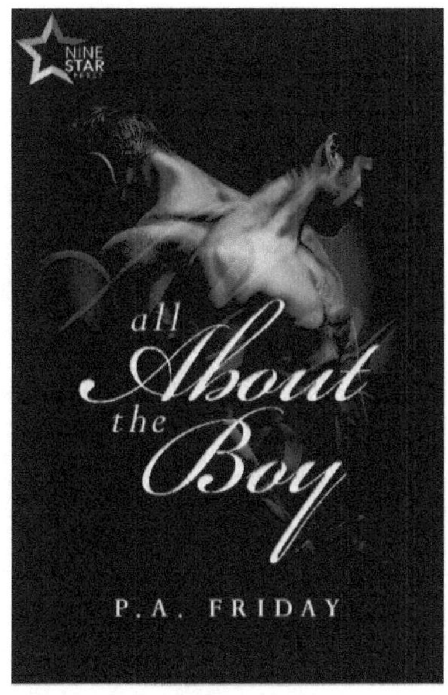

Connect with NineStar Press

www.ninestarpress.com

www.facebook.com/ninestarpress

www.facebook.com/groups/NineStarNiche

www.twitter.com/ninestarpress

www.tumblr.com/blog/ninestarpress